BRICKS AND ANCHORS

BRICKS AND ANCHORS

Stories
by

JON LONGHI

manic d press
san francisco

Also by Jon Longhi:

Zucchini and other stories

ISBN 0-916397-12-2

cover art: John Borruso

manic d press
box 410804
san francisco, ca 94141

CONTENTS

BRICKS AND ANCHORS

MY REPUTATION

When I was in the army my platoon would send me into the bad neighborhoods to score drugs for the boys. I just had a reputation for not getting ripped off. I'd go into a slum up to a row house that looked like roach heaven. In the sleazy living room that smelled of dirty laundry would be a nervous pencil face dude with bad shakes. His fat biker chick would be plopped on the couch one eye keen, the other staring off into space at nothing, filthy baby perched on her side with snot dripping down off its chin and pencil face asks, "Do you want a drink?" Fuck no! Not from you Manson clones, just give me the drugs and I'll get the fuck out of this shit hole.

Pencil face starts to gibber and spit and vomits up some green shit that slides under the couch and begins to dissolve roaches. The biker chick pulls the plug out of the baby which is really an inflatable doll with fake snot and it flies around the room with a loud farting noise. That's when I realize they've slipped me a Mickey. How, I don't know. Luckily I'm carrying a rod and wave it round the air screaming "I'm gonna shoot!" hoping they don't find out it's got no bullets. The biker chick turns out to be Curly Joe in drag and starts beating me with a dildo whining "Wise Guy! Wise Guy!" Pencil face has got the shakes so bad he's just a blurred area.

I grab a sheet of acid and a quarter pound of reefer off the coffee table and high tail it for the fire escape, roaches snapping at my heels. Curly Joe is lighting farts and blowing them at me like a flame thrower. The green shit under the couch catches fire and blows up big as nitro leveling the surrounding two blocks. Pencil face is vibrating so fast he caves in to a black hole as Curly Joe shoots into orbit using his flaming asshole as a rocket booster. Burned the zits off my back but at least I escaped with the drugs and my reputation intact.

JOE CANDYBAR

Joe Candybar driving a big red Sedan cross the bad-lands drunk out of his mind. He's going all the way to L.A. to live with the rest of the freaks and has been sucking on the Jim Beam since Patterson, New Jersey. In Warsaw, Wisconsin he hit a dairy cow but just kept on going. Then in the endless grass hills of South Dakota he started on a permanent weave. More crank made the two roads turn back into one and Joe was so happy he made himself another drink.

Acne covers his face. In the heat of the day he'll stop and eat a road pizza off the white line, skunk or coon, some-times even a stray dog; he can't wait to head south and chomp on some armadillo. After five days on the road without sleep-ing a peep Joe is running out of crank and has to down Budweisers steady to keep the twitch out of his back, every campground he passes reminds him of sleep. He doesn't know where he is in Wyoming but this place sure is big.

Joe is completely lost and no longer cares where he was going. At least there are liquor stores here too, if not much else. Low gray hills, red gullies, mountains that rise out of nothing. Joe has forgotten where his car is and is running into an endless plain of scrub. The scattered bushes and grass roll on for hundreds of miles interrupted occasionally by a cowboy on a horse. Three days without seeing a city and Joe forgot what time was. America is incredibly large and he is shrinking ever smaller inside of it. Spirits of Indians rise out of the rust hills. Joe disappears. A dance begins. Sparks leap from the fire. All things fall to fragments. Thirty years later Joe's car is a rusted hulk in the Nevada desert. He runs on all fours through the cider hills, eating coyotes.

I had just gotten back from Vegas and was waiting for a local in this slimy rundown Greyhound station in East L.A. when the oily burrito I had eaten for lunch reached critical mass and melted down into one of the messiest diarrheas I've ever had. By the time I had gotten out of the can I'd missed my bus so I figured fuck it and began to hoof it through the slum. It was one of those flat primitive neighborhoods that festers nameless beneath the L.A. heat and smog. Nothing but winos and junkies everywhere you looked. Seedy flophouse hotels with sagging floorboards and burnt out neon signs. Every other store was a liquor store. I had only walked about three blocks when a street person asked if I could spare any change. I threw him a quarter and kept walking. He didn't think it was enough and told me so.

"Man, I know you got more money than that. Nice looking guy like you gotta have money. Man, you need me, this is a rough neighborhood, you need me to walk you through it." He kept tagging after me, tugging on my coat sleeve. Finally I turned around and said, "Look, man, all I got's is twenty bucks and it's gotta last me three days."

"Well, I can make change man, give me the bill and I'll break it. Man, I know everyone around here." He waved over two of his bum friends from a nearby street corner. One of them stank of sour molasses. All three started tugging on my jacket and begging for money. I sped up my pace but they clung like remoras. In the next block they were joined by four more winos. Now I had a regular crowd hanging on me screaming, "Gimme de bill, I'll break it," tugging and grabbing on me like I was fucking Jesus or something. I would have been scared shitless if I wasn't shitless already and finally I ran out into a busy street of traffic, cars swerving all around, a pickup truck squealed to a stop right in front of me and I said, "Look, man, you gotta help me," and jumped in the back of his truck. He peeled out. Five blocks down he jammed on his breaks and screamed, "Get the fuck out of my truck!" I did.

About a half hour later I was waiting at a bus stop for another local. A bum was foraging through a garbage can for something to eat. He found a chicken carcass and began picking green fungus off it. Me and him got to talking. "You know I'm a bum but I'm honest," he said. He went on to tell me that he had found a bag of money beside the road that morning. It was the find of a lifetime but he was going to give it back because there was a name and address stenciled on the side of the bag. He pulled it out of his greasy coat and sure enough, there it was, a little canvas sack with what looked like a few thousand dollars in it. He went back to picking fungus off his chicken and I just stood there waiting for my bus, thinking about what money means.

JIM JANE

Jim Jane slept with everyone. He was Mr. Smooth, wrote the Book of Love, and How To Pick Up Chicks, knew every trick and all of them worked. Of course he was good looking. Short brown hair above a perfect complexion, classic features, nice arms, lean body. Women liked it.

He had lived in Delaware all his life, knew everyone, was popular. Maybe that's why his first semester in college he stopped going to classes after four days and just started partying every night of the week. It was easy and there was always something going on. He was talented, played good rock and roll guitar so the chicks flew to him like magnets. One hell of a fall. But come winter session first term's grades hit home like D-Day with twice the flack and he knew he was only at U. of D. for another six weeks before he got the boot.

He had decided with his parents that it would be best if they shipped him away to an electronics school in Alabama where there weren't any drugs and most of all no one he knew. It was an intensive two-year trade school that only gave him one week off a year. That oughta keep him straight. But this gave Jim just a month and a half to party in the place he'd spent all his life in. A long good-bye with his own private dorm room; studying was no longer an issue.

Jim wanted to sleep with every girl he'd ever known in Delaware before he left. He almost succeeded. One hundred and thirty-two in six weeks. That's 3.14 per day. At first it just seemed like a good luck streak. A roll. But soon it became apparent that this was something bigger. More monumental. He was slacking if he hadn't picked one up by eleven a.m. Girls in the dining halls for breakfast should be more cautious. Lunch was always an easy score. At dinner I once saw him make four dates spread out over three consecutive hours.

Whenever you went to visit him, there was one in the bed. He even converted a lesbian. A politically-correct bull dyke named Edie Jarvis, who we called Cookie Jarvis. She was all over him before he even said a word just on the power of eye contact. They fucked seven times that night. "Once I just touched her and she came," Jim said. Edie's been straight ever since.

Fat girls, skinny girls, white ones, black ones, models, typists, ditch diggers, whores. He was a bare-assed streak through the population. At parties he'd leave with a blond early when everyone was still sober, come back around ten, snag a brunette in the weave and loud talk, and still make it back around three to get that last perm-headed frou-frou who wouldn't even remember him. Some sisters and girlfriends got together and compared notes, and though Jim always rated A+, he had to be stopped. Why, the boy had more virgins than fingers and maybe even toes. They organized a sort of lynch mob to track him down and bring him to celibacy or at least monogamy, but they could never find him, he was always off sleeping with some girl. He managed to stay one woman ahead of justice, until the McLaren sisters and the field hockey team kicked down his dorm room door. But he was already on the plane headed for Alabama. Three months later he was married.

STEROIDS

When I was in high school I dealt steroids. Well, they weren't real steroids, just Geritols. But all the ignoramuses on the football team believed in them, and would come up to me like, "Man, those were great! Last month I put three inches on my chest." Most drugs are ninety percent idea. Plus I knew all these guys were working out so much anyway they were bound to put on muscle naturally. So that year I made a lot of bucks at it. Just figured Geritols would be safer. What are they gonna bust me for? Felonious distribution of vitamins in a high school? But the football team, the jocks, and body builders were a pretty big and dangerous interest group to rip off.

That summer some guy shows up, weighs 350 with a body like the Hulk, big macho dude with blond hair. And he's been taking real steroids, and he sees my big red tablets and says, "Wait a second, Dianabols are little blue pills." So him and the quarterback of the football team confront me in the locker room one afternoon. I play the fool. "Oh no, man! Sorry, I never seen Dianabols before. I been getting these pills from some guy in Seattle and he musta been burning me all along." They thought I was an okay dude and besides, I'm a big guy so they thought I believed in them too and wouldn't lie. I got off easy.

Later that spring two guys show up selling real hormones. They got some male nurse over at Mercy Hospital stealing them by the case, pill forms, injectables, you name it. These two guys got a closet full at home, probably like thousands of dollars worth. Well, that year our football team turns into something out of Gulliver's Travels. So many guys are turning into Superman word gets to the Millstown Cougars, the football team in the next town over, and they track down the two dudes and start buying from them too. Only they sell them a different kind of steroid. A kind they're not exactly sure what it's going to do. Three or four months later it turns out these are female steroids, estrogens. We find out cause the Millstown Cougars start growing tits! You got this whole team of big hulky guys with soft faces and flabby cow titties.

15

One day the Cougars come over to our school to beat up the two steroid dealers. But the dealers are good friends of the local team quarterback and we kind of have this showdown in the gym. On one side of the basketball court you have this group of big, burly, man steroid dudes, and on the other side you got this team of strong but kind of feminine, smooth dudes with breasts. Our quarterback just walks over to the Cougars' quarterback and yells, "Hey Tits!" and pinches his big breast. I thought the Cougar guy was going to throw a punch and he really looked like he might, but he didn't. Our quarterback finally said, "It's not our fault you all are idiots." Both teams stared each other down real vicious for about five minutes, but finally the Cougars shuffled out in defeat. Only we never let them forget it at the football games that fall. Sitting in the stands yelling things like, "He'd pass the ball but he keeps hitting himself in the face with his tits!" and "Ya can't tell the football team from the cheerleaders!"

We had been shopping all day in Manhattan and I bought a really nice jacket with leather elbow and shoulder patches that cost me a hundred bucks. Then we got on the subway going downtown to Soho to see a show. The train pulled off into the dark tunnel. We sat at the end, by the door, and the car was nearly full, winding down of rush hour traffic with a lot of commuters still on their way out. I read the sign on the metal wall that said you weren't supposed to cross between cars while the train was moving. But sure enough, someone was on the crosswalk and they paused for a second at the door, looking through the window checking the car out. It was the most menacing face I have ever seen. The door slid open and he stepped in. He had obviously been a very big man before he started doing drugs. What looked like a steady year or two's use had burned off all his body fat and a lot of the muscle as well. His skin and shape was shrunken and tight, the skeleton slowly showing its angles. But he was still big. A lot bigger than me. His face was contorted in a hideous grimace of such intensity that the skin was squeezed a raw purple. His fists were purple too, clenched and reclenched so hard that the blood welled up in them like angry clouds. His jaw moved frantically, grinding his teeth down to little stumps. The greasy raincoat, the filthy jeans he had pulled out of a trash heap. But his face. I have never seen such a pure concentration of anger, hatred, and pain. Violence boiled through his whole body, rising on waves of the drug. And he was standing right there in front of me. I did what everyone else in the car did, I tried to ignore him.

"You!" he screamed, right in my face.

"Well, um," I stuttered. "You, uh, talking to me?"

"You scumfuck dick brained white ass motherfucker. This fuckin' coat you're wearing! Probably cost more than I make in a shittin' week!"

"Well, uh," I just shrugged. What could I say? I'm sorry I'm white? I'm sorry I'm privileged and middle class? I'm sorry I have money?

"You fucking cunt lipped faggot assed motherfucker. I'm gonna kill you! I'm gonna kill you!"

I'm thinking, well now, you've got nineteen dollars and ninety-five cents worth of karate under your belt, you went to two lessons. Use the four moves you learned on him. This is it. Man to man. The big showdown. I gotta kill him.

"You!" he screamed at the person next to me. "You fucking turd breath douche bag son of a..."

After he yelled at and threatened to kill the two people I was with, he yelled at the people next to them and slowly worked his way down our side of the car and along the back, then up the other side till he was finally back to the door he had come in through. Black people in the back of the car were hiding their faces, embarrassed as hell by this guy, I could hear them thinking, "Shut up. Go away. White people hate us enough without assholes like you coming along and fucking it up for the rest of us."

The madman stood staring out the window, his hand on the door. Finally, I thought, he's yelled at everyone on the train now, he's gotten it out of his system, and now he's going to go away.

He spun around and stared at me with pure mutilation in his eyes.

"You!" he screamed. "I remember you. And now I'm gonna really kill you!"

Me and my two friends flexed our muscles. The showdown again. Man to man. But we were scared shitless of the dude. The train stopped. The doors hissed open. All three of us got up and ran for the exit. And there, standing on the platform like a miracle, were three huge black lady transit workers. Each of them must of weighed over two hundred and fifty pounds.

"Help us!" we screamed. "This guy's trying to kill us." They looked at the scene for a second, taking it all in. Then the biggest of them said in a thick Bronx accent, "Well there's three of you and only one of him, why don't you kick his ass?"

"We don't want to kick his ass," I shrieked, "We don't want to kick anybody's ass. Now just call a cop or something please."

"Okay," she said, lifting a bullhorn to her mouth, "But are you really sure you don't want to kick his ass?"

"Yes!"

She called out some numbers into the bullhorn and two transit cops came running. They grabbed the madman who ended up leaving peacefully without a struggle. As we were walking away one of the big transit girls said, "You know, that's a nice jacket you're wearing. You probly spent more on that jacket than I make in a week. It really woulda been okay if you'd kicked his ass. We wouldna told nobody."

As I walked to the turnstiles I noticed how much they looked like prison bars.

SLIM WINS

"Paging Mr. Reiter. Mr. Slim Reiter, white courtesy telephone."

Slim pushed back from the chromium bar where he had been playing quarter poker. Jarvis the bartender had been tightening him up with stiff drinks all afternoon. Vegas. His kind of town. The flashing lights and mirrors hurt his bloodshot eyes. Old women pouring quarters into slot machines with such a metronomic regularity that they appeared to be machines themselves. The Frontier was a nice casino, much more neighborly than Caesar's Palace uptown. That trash tower was nothing but a poodle joint, wanted to see your movie star before they'd treat ya human, even made ya pay for drinks while you were throwing away your money at their tables. But when it came right down to it, this whole town was nothing but a monument to trash.

Slim took the white receiver from the cocktail waitress. "Yeah."

"Slim, this is Freddy. Freddy Squirm."

"Cookie Pus, how ya doing?"

"Slim, watch your ass. Guido's gunning for you. You been paying too slow on those bad blackjack bets. Rumor says it's a good thing all the lake beds in Nevada are dry or you'd be doing some heavy walking at the bottom of one."

Jesus. Not Guido. Father Guido they called him. A four hundred pound Mafioso don with no arms or legs. He was a thalidomide baby born into one of the most powerful gangster families. His 200+ I.Q. allowed him to take over as 'The Head' after his father, Old Man Guido, was gunned down by the Sunshine Boys. Not even the death threats of his family had kept school children from taunting the young handicapped Guido and calling him "Flipper." This had emotionally scarred him beyond repair and he had learned to love acts of sadistic violence that involved dismemberment as if these were some act of revenge against the non-handicapped world. Now he sat like a pile of flab in a penthouse atop one of the largest casinos in Las Vegas where beautiful showgirls stuffed grapes and chocolates into his mouth.

Slim owed him a lot of money. A lot of money. For a

blackjack winning streak that had gone bad. At the time Slim had been so drunk he wouldn't accept it and just kept betting into the void hoping he'd run into Lady Luck again. He didn't. He'd been dodging those debts ever since then. Buying time with bad excuses to try and win back some of the dough. But the jacks were down all over town. Slim had big tabs in a string of joints along the Strip and it was just a matter of time before the bone breakers caught up with him. He looked down at his clothes and thought about what it would be like to buy pants that only had one leg. Or maybe he wouldn't have to buy pants at all.

Down on his luck and going nowhere. Thirty-two years old with not a thing to show for it. He only owned one good suit and it was going seedy. Even Judy, the only girl he'd ever really had, who he was engaged to marry, had broken up with him because he was a chronic gambler. Maybe it was time to cash in the chips. Go back to San Francisco and sell insurance with his brother. Yeah, that was it. Get an honest job. He'd give it a shot at being a straight Joe.

He said good-bye to Cookie Pus and caught a cab to the bus depot. There he bought a one-way to San Francisco. As the bus rolled out into the cactus-covered hills Slim noticed that a huge flock of crows was flying out with them, apparently abandoning the city. When they were deep in the Mojave Desert the whole earth shook like an earthquake and cracks spiderwebbed the road. Thunder blew out the bus windows. Slim turned to look back at Vegas but the whole city was engulfed in a reddish cloud. Then he realized what had happened. Someone at the U.S. Government Nuclear Testing Site must have miscalculated on the power of their latest firecracker. Now Trash City was burning. All those slot machines and roulette wheels melting. Slim felt in his pockets. They were full of quarters.

PUMPKIN MAN

For a year the Pumpkin Man lived in our ratty old house. He used to drift about the dim dirty rooms like a quiet island of protoplasm. MSG and carbohydrates had ruined his life, mutated him with flab and cellulite into an outcast from the social mainstream. He would sit in his dark room all day jerking off to pornos on his VCR, generating foul smells. The room was a thick tangled nest in which it was impossible to separate his possessions from the garbage. To an outsider it all looked like trash. Stacks of paper were everywhere with coffee and cola spilled on them, piles of dog-eared sci-fi novels and stained Playboys, peanut shells and candy wrappers. It was a breeding ground for silverfish.

Sometimes when I passed his room I would see him sitting there in an easy chair for hours staring at something in his lap. For a long time I figured he was just reading. But it turned out he was writing "God is Bogus" over and over again on tiny stickers. For hours on end he would sit there writing and rewriting this phrase. He produced over a hundred thousand of these stickers. Packs of five hundred were given to his friends to distribute to all their friends. For months Pumpkin Man went around to yard sales and through all his friends' magazines tearing out the Business Reply mail cards from the advertisements. A "God is Bogus" sticker was pasted to each of these cards and they were mailed out to thousands of randomly picked addresses across the United States. Everywhere you went around town, on telephone poles, in store windows, even above the urinals in the Deerpark Tavern, was pasted a "God is Bogus" sticker.

Something had to be done. This had gone too far. So me and some of my friends got together and we wrote up ten thousand stickers which read: "Pumpkin Man is Bogus." And then we stuck them all over town.

Possibly the oddest thing about Pumpkin Man was how he ate. He only owned one cooking utensil - a large stew pot which always sat on a burner on the stove. At the beginning of the week, he would throw about ten pounds of beef into this pot and boil the fuck out of it. Then he would eat some of it and leave the rest just sitting on the cold stove. The next day he would come back, throw some pasta in with the greenish beef, boil it until they became an indistinguishable mass, eat some, and leave the rest in the pot to ferment. Over the course of the week he would throw in whatever came to mind: lettuce, corn, lentils, anchovies, and boil it all into some generic union. In the whole of the year he lived there he never once refrigerated the contents of the pot. We had to be very careful about leaving any of our food lying around, because even if it was rotten Pumpkin Man would steal it and throw it into his pot. All things went into that pot, the living and dead, edible and inedible, and out of that mixing place Pumpkin Man drew most of his bland sustenance. The other forty percent of his diet was made up of sour cream and onion potato chips. He ate four and a half meals a day and this is what it took to keep his dough boy figure.

Pumpkin Man did not do drugs, nor did he drink. He was very shy and in crowds he seldom said a word. I'm sure he was a virgin. But he was at all the parties, in every bar, at all public gatherings, silently drifting among the jabbering cliques like a ghost whale. He was everywhere and yet no place, everyone and yet no one, in short he was a mixing place like the pot he ate from, a silent stew of all things, the fat round virgin who had aborted God.

CRASH

The ship had crash landed who the fuck knows where and all the food stuffs went up with the life pods, my comic book collection and everything else, a neon purple smear on the dark red landscape as we ran behind some boulders and hid like prehistoric cavemen. Just before the flames hit the nuclear piles this gigantic but peaceful looking humanoid runs up and stomps them out. While he goes to get a broom and dust pan we run up to see if there's anything to salvage. A complete wreck. Some monstrous toddlers see us and violently repulsed, they race toward us and stomp Lieutenant Lineck to raspberry jam. So we hauled ass into this church that's just a few hundred yards away. By the time we make it into a sewer hole Corollson and Nula are little red circles too. Imagine the night we spent freezing our asses off among yards of alien excrement.

By the time the four suns rose at dawn we were starving. We decided to risk a run into the cathedral-like kitchen. Unfortunately the only receptacle we could gain entry to was the garbage can. Better to eat garbage than shit. After we had spelunked through acres of rot we finally found some crumbs that didn't have ferocious little penguins all over them. The scanner said they were edible. Tasted a bit like tennis shoes but they weren't bad with the bit of ketchup I had snagged before ejecting.

About a half hour after the meal we started farting something awful. It got worse and worse and pretty soon everyone was blowing a steady stream of wet ones, we sounded like a bunch of tubas. Then Booba's belly starts to get big and round. Motherfucker looks pregnant. Then we all swell up to nine months. Booba's bloated up big as a weather balloon and farting so hard he lifts up off the ground and explodes. I see what's happening and pull out my knife. As Babs pops all over me I slice my belly from here to there. A big wind blows out the wound and I'm jetted back against the side of the can. Everyone else farted to death while all the penguins laughed at them.

A RUMOR MOVING THROUGH THE CROWD

Roth Forjic was the only person I ever knew who was allergic to his own skin. Sweating would make him break out in a rash and to help alleviate this condition he took frequent vinegar baths. These often left him smelling like a salad bar.

He had a mind like an intricate biological computer. No fact escaped him, no matter how small or insignificant. Conversations, labels, telephone numbers, birth dates, everything was lurking in the wrinkles of his brain. Statistics and gossip were his specialties. He could tell you how many people had whooping cough in New Hampshire in 1968, and what the exact circumference of Catherine the Great's vagina was. He spent hours in libraries memorizing insignificant facts, and had quit smoking pot in high school to make his powers of recollection even more formidable.

The most dangerous items in his archives were his countless tidbits of gossip. He absorbed them like a magnetic field. Once they were logged and stored everyone found out what a short distance it is from the brain to the mouth. He just loved to spread that knowledge around, no matter what kind of havoc it caused. In fact he seemed to relish spreading it where it would cause the most damage. And when people came to him in rages with their relationships and jobs destroyed, he would innocently protest, "But what did I say that wasn't true?" This logic cost him his front teeth one night but not even that stopped the tireless flow of secrets. He never seemed to realize that the truth in the wrong place can be an extremely destructive thing. Some things depend on lies. But he never saw that. "Everything should be known," he would say, and off he would go to spread his secrets, rumors, and half truths with a voraciousness equalled only by the news media.

He was all the more dangerous because he was one of the most social people that ever existed. He was at every party, every bar, every concert, every opening. If he wasn't invited he would go anyway. And all the time his ears were open and his mouth running. Around him collapsed relationships, careers, and friendships.

No one could get back at him. He had no vices. Loathed drugs. Drank but rarely to excess. He hated sex and in fact considered it a complete waste of time. The idea of love or a close relationship never seemed to occur to him. Never could he understand why people wasted so much time and energy on such insane couplings. All of his affairs were in complete order. He never borrowed or loaned. A self-contained universe, a complete narcissist to the last. Nobody could get even a shred of scandal on him.

After years of work we did find one good story on Roth. In high school he had once taken a shit that was bigger around than a Coke can. It was so big it wouldn't flush down and literally had to be shoveled out of the toilet. That pile became somewhat of a local legend and for years afterward people told tales of the "Forjic Turd." But unfortunately the potency of this story as a social weapon was limited. We needed something more. But he was wiped clean.

And then his gossiping took an even more vicious turn. He decided that reality wasn't interesting enough and began to make up rumors about people. Some of them were real gems. Like one about this spoiled girl we all knew. He told everyone that her father had arranged at birth for her to be married to a rich Arab sheik. The whole agreement depended on her still being a virgin on the wedding night. So when she broke her hymen while horseback riding, her father who was a plastic surgeon sewed it back together. We all knew the rumor wasn't true but we spread it anyway.

After a while everyone got so pissed off at Forjic for spreading lies that they began to make up false rumors about him. We told everyone that he was gay and for five years had been the private gigolo of a fat sleazy hairball of a businessman. All day long Forjic would lounge around the millionaire's villa fanning himself. Six times a day the fat smelly pig would butt fuck Forjic as he nonchalantly read the World Almanac and quoted statistics. Supposedly Roth ended the relationship and stomped out in a huff when the businessman refused to fill the swimming pool with vinegar.

Now Roth Forjic is moving outwards, becoming bigger. He's joined a sperm bank and soon you'll start seeing tiny replicas of him walking around. Little sexless computer brained gossips that smell of vinegar. They shall inherit the earth. I once told a friend that some day Roth will gossip too much, spread himself too thin, he'll disintegrate into a mass of conversation, a spreading of secrets, and afterwards will only exist as a rumor moving through the crowd.

MERCEDES BENDER

Taj was starting this new job and had to show up at four a.m. He was paranoid about being able to stay awake so me and Fritz took him out partying to keep him alert. Fritz borrowed his parents Mercedes Benz without telling them and we headed for the back roads driving 110, downing beers the whole way. Four joints and a six pack later it's only 9:30 and Taj is already having trouble keeping his eyes open. Fritz decides to wake him up by pulling into a dirt pit and spinning donuts, getting dust and mud all over the nice white trim. Then we squeal back onto the road and leave a hundred feet of blistered rubber. I'm laughing so hard I pop open another Bud and fill a bowl. For a while Fritz starts driving with no lights on, swerving all over the road till me and Taj experience complete bladder failure and beg him to stop. When he turns on the lights, there's a raccoon spooked on the white line, and like he's some big animal lover, he swerves and we go into a spin, Taj puking all over the nice creme upholstery, and the car grinds over some big rocks on the roadside and from the sounds of tearing metal we know when we finally stop we're going nowhere. For about five minutes Fritz has a complete freak out nervous breakdown. "Oh God, what am I gonna do! My parents don't even know I've got the car! They're gonna freak. I'm dead! They'll cut me up in little pieces. Mother Fuck! How could this have happened? We weren't fucking around that much!" Taj was already asleep in the back seat. There were little pastel stains all around his head.

I know it's going to take major body work but Fritz insists that we can fix it that night before his parents find out, if we can just get our hands on some tools. So we wake up Taj and tell him it's time to start walking. Well, we walk for about five miles and don't see a gas station or any human habitation of any kind, just trees, empty fields, and darkness. Finally we come across one lonely farm house out in the middle of nowhere and knock on the door. The old couple who answer it look at us like we just stepped out of *A Clockwork Orange*. We explain that our car has broken down (which only confirms this first impression) and that we need to borrow some tools. The old geezer hands me a screwdriver. Thanks. Like what are we gonna do with this? Maybe we can jack the car up with it. So we give him back his screwdriver and walk back to the car rather dejectedly.

On the way, Taj keeps complaining about how tired he is and finally hits upon a cure for his exhaustion. He'll drop a hit of acid. No sooner said than done. By the time we get back to the car things are already getting stringy for him and there's two police cruisers parked around the Benz. It's not that big a deal but they pull us all into the police station to report the accident. While the desk guy is writing up Fritz, Taj has a schizophrenic episode and I have to stop him from eating a potted plant in the reception room. Then the cops bring us back and drop us by the car in the middle of nowhere.

Fritz still thinks he can get away without telling his parents, but it's hopeless. Taj is worried about being late for work but at least he's not tired anymore. Suddenly he runs off into a field chasing after "the bird of truth." So we hike back to the farmhouse, wake up the old couple again, and use their phone to call Fritz's Mom. She shows up in a matching white Benz, pissed as hell. It takes about forty-five minutes to drive back to the city and she goes off the whole time about how we're basically shit, a bunch of irresponsible bastards, drug-taking hoodlums, dumb thugs, you know, the complete third degree, and the whole time Taj is in the back seat talking about how he's a washing machine. And Fritz's Mom is getting freaked out because she doesn't understand what's going on with him. Around the city limits Taj goes into his spin cycle.

DEAD PEOPLE

I'm twenty-six years old and I've never seen a dead person. I'm happy to say I haven't known too many people who've died. A couple of years ago a friend of mine was killed in an automobile accident but his body was cremated and there was no open viewing. When my grandfather died, I was in my early twenties and I was too broke to fly cross-country for the funeral.

When I was in college a friend of mine, David, had also never seen a dead person. We got to talking about it and decided that it was very important that we see a corpse as soon as possible. As far along as we were in our adult development, it might be too traumatic for us to see a stiff unexpectedly at this point. It might really freak us out and drive us crazy, especially if it were a relative or friend, and we were the first ones to find the body. Sure, we had seen dead people in the movies and on TV, but TV isn't real life. So we went out in search of Death.

We went to the local hospital first, but our school was in a small town so there was no one dead there that day. Next we went to the police station. They just laughed at us. So we went to Drake Hall. Drake Hall was the medical science building on campus, a huge labyrinthian structure of twisting dark hallways and silent classrooms. We went on a Saturday afternoon so the place was nearly deserted. Just a few students reading in the study lounges here and there. We were looking for the Physical Therapy Department, which supposedly had cadavers for the grad students' dissection and anatomy courses. Only we couldn't find it anyplace. For two hours we walked around those twisting, winding halls reading the plaques on doors until we were completely lost.

Finally, in the basement, we asked directions from an Oriental student who led us to two huge steel refrigeration doors. We knew that on the other side of that impenetrable wall lay the cold landscapes of death. Only the doors were locked. We banged on them but no one answered. Obviously. So we bummed around the empty Physical Therapy Department for about forty-five minutes until a professor happened by. We explained to him that we desperately needed to see a dead person. He jokingly replied that there were plenty of dead professors in the Physical Therapy Department but once he found out we were serious, he thought we were a couple of weirdos and had us thrown out of the building. As the campus police officer was pushing us out the door we pleaded with him, "But wait! We've got to see death!"

"Sorry, not today," he said, and slammed the door in our faces. Dejectedly, we walked back to the world of the living.

I think all this goes back to the first funeral I ever went to. It was my great-grandfather's wake in Wisconsin. I was only six years old, and me and my mother flew out on a plane. On the flight I spilled seven Coca Colas. Two in my own lap, one in my mother's, and four on businessmen who only sat next to us for a short amount of time. We stayed at the family's cabin on Lake Ochachee. There was a horrendous blizzard going on and everything was soft, white, and rounded, silent under six inches of snow. The only heat in the place was from a squat pot-bellied stove which my mother stoked with fuel until the iron glowed bright red. I remember worrying all night about what would happen if the heat went away and I did not understand what had happened to Grandpa. I wondered if I would be able to talk to him at his funeral.

Two days later, at the viewing in Milwaukee, it was unseasonably hot. All the snow had melted and it was a bright sunny day. The graveyard was a vibrant green, with happy little white tombstones shining beneath the blue sky. Everyone on my mother's side of the family was there. It was a regular reunion. My cousins, Tony and Chris, were there too. They were also in the mid-range of their single digit years and we began rough-housing on the lawn and calling each other names. Grandma scolded us for getting our nice clothes dirty. Why was everyone wearing black? Why was everyone so upset? It was a beautiful sunny day.

When everyone was walking by this big box, me and Tony and Chris began throwing dirt clods at them. One exploded right on Uncle Rick's fez. Then Aunt Char had a conniption fit and threw us out of the funeral. We had to stand over by the cars next to this big black thing that looked like a station wagon. We didn't care, it was nice to get away from

31

those sourpusses. The three of us began to play in the dirt. The old people began to mess in the dirt too. I just remember looking back at all those people dressed in black, huddled together weeping on such a beautiful day.

What a fucking night. I get home after a ball busting ten hour shift wanting to do nothing but die, and the place has no heat. Mid-December and I'm looking at my breath in the living room. It's been off all day but nobody else in the building has gotten their head out of their ass long enough to do something about it. Well, you know me, I just put a little Vaseline on my edges and slide on through. Don't expect me to lead but I'll follow ya right to the cliff's edge. But now suddenly everything's my responsibility.

I call the landlord's emergency maintenance number. Some drunk old woman answers the phone. At first I think she can't understand English but it soon becomes apparent that she's just too sauced to recognize any rudiments of communication. I can see this dame, pushing retirement in an E-cup bra, curlers and tattoos with a can of cheap beer surgically attached to one hand. Finally she understands our heat is off. She doesn't want to deal with it and tells me I have a wrong number.

"Look I know this is the right number, you already told me you're Mr. Scarface's emergency service."

She refers me to another number. It's to a room at the Tequila Sunrise Hotel. I know the place, a sleazy whore dive next to the porns on the highway. The type of place where cheap floozies with nicotine breath drink cheap bourbon with pot bellied salesmen.

Squeaky answers the phone. He's drunk. When I tell him we have no heat he starts laughing. He only stops giggling long enough to tell me he can't do anything and hangs up in my face. I figure it's time to go straight to the top of the ladder. I call the landlord at his residential number. His answering machine has a taped message: "Whoever you are I don't care, stop calling me, stop bothering me, I don't live here anymore. If you got any questions talk to my lawyer. Thank you."

After the beep I tell him we need heat. Just as I'm hanging up I could swear I hear someone laughing at the other end. There's also no answer at his office number, his lawyer's number, his children's number, or on his car phone.

Luckily I have space heaters. Two of them. They're

called heat logs and they look like little turds that turn orange when you plug them in. Unfortunately they're three pronged so I spent a half hour foraging for adapters. Eureka! I found two. As soon as I turned on the heaters every light in the apartment went out. This, of course, meant that I had to find our fusebox in the dreaded basement. The basement of our building is one of those filth choked nether rooms of Hell, filled to the moldy gills with cobwebs, cockroaches, and psychopaths. You can imagine my delight at discovering we had no flashlight. So I opened the storm doors and crawled into this dust bowl purgatory armed with nothing but a disposable plastic lighter. It put out a feeble aura of illumination that did little for my sense of security. There was still enough darkness in that basement to hold the entire cast of *Night of the Living Dead.*

Just when I got to the deepest, blackest part of the cellar, eeeouch! the lighter got too hot to hold. So I had to stand there in the killer filled darkness waiting for it to cool down enough for me to light it again. This wasn't helped by my roommates who stood back by the storm doors yelling, "He's in there! Jason's gonna get you! Ha ha ha ha!" before they broke into a choral rendition of the theme song from *Psycho.* I found the box and put the fuses in. Our apartment burst into light. Unfortunately my roommate had left his electric guitar plugged in when the power went off. Now the amplifier let out an unearthly shriek of feedback which crescendoed louder and louder till the fuse box sputtered blue in my face and the entire building plunged back into darkness. So we went upstairs, unplugged the guitar, and I crawled back across the dirt floor of the basement and put in new fuses again. Finally I could relax.

There was frost on the dirty dishes in the sink, but at least we had light. We were slowly returning to the twentieth century. To celebrate, me and my roommates sat down and began to get stoned. I realized I was filthy from crawling around in the basement and hopped into the shower. The warm water felt good on my skin. I stayed in for a long time, till all the hot water was gone. As soon as I stepped out dripping onto the mat my roommates plugged in the stereo and all the lights went out again. So I started to fill another tub and went crawling back through the scummy basement.

By the time I got to the fusebox my wet hair was full of cobwebs and dead potato bugs. While I was fiddling with the switches and my roommates (brave souls that they are) were cringing back by the storm doors shouting words of encouragement to me, a cop came to the front door of our apartment and noticing it was unlatched, walked right in. This was the only lucky coincidence in the whole string of disasters. My roommates had left the weed and bongs strewn all over the living room floor and had the lights been working she would have obviously seen them and busted us. As it was the place was pitch black and when she could neither see nor hear anyone she walked out and eventually found her way to the storm doors. As soon as she left our apartment I finished screwing in the fuse and the lights went back on. When I made it back to the storm doors with grime all over my cheeks I found myself face to face with a lady cop.

"Do you live in this first floor apartment?" she asked.

"That depends."

"On what?"

"On what you want with the person who lives there."

"Do you own a big dog?"

Ahhh. Sigh of relief. The previous tenant of the apartment had owned an Irish wolfhound big as a pony. The only pet we had was a piranha we fed mice to.

"No, that was the guy who lived here before us. What happened, did his dog eat a little kid or something?"

"No, We found him wandering on a country road a few miles south of here and we wanted to return him to his owner."

"Big black dog that drools a lot?"

"Yeah. He's drooling all over the back seat of my squad car right now. Plus he shit all over the back seat of the car they brought him in, and urinated on the side of the Sergeant's desk down at the station."

"Yeah, that's Orson. He always did act like the world was his litterbox. Look, the dog's name is Orson. But you're gonna have a big problem with him."

"What?"

"He only responds to commands in French."

The cop got pissed. She accused me of lying and stomped out in a huff. But it was the truth. The guy who owned the dog was an exchange student from Cannes. He had raised the dog in his native language. I tried to explain this to the cop, but she refused to believe me.

As she climbed into her car the dog leaned over the front seat and a tongue big as a wash cloth slobbered over half her face. She began cussing up a storm, wiping off her dripping chin with a Kleenex and the dog's breath! Ugh! I've smelled sweeter assholes. Then she fixed me with a venomous look and hissed, "We'll remember this lack of cooperation down at the station. You just better watch yourself in this town." There was a squealing of tires and she was gone.

When we got inside I saw I had left the water running too long and the tub had overflowed across the bathroom floor. Since the apartment had reached equilibrium with the outside world, this was already freezing over like a skating rink. I said "Fuck it" and went to bed. My bedroom was toasty as an igloo. I decided I'd risk just one of the space heaters. Soon it was glowing a pretty thermal orange as I huddled over it in a blanket. When the feeling returned to my fingers and toes I realized it was time to collapse. I reached for the glass of water on my nightstand and washed down a valium. As I was setting the glass back down, don't ask me how, but it slipped out of my hand, and as it was still half full, a huge curve of water opened out in mid-air, and landed right on the space heater. My little heat log was instantly transformed into a hornets' nest of sizzling arcs and tiny explosions. By the time it had finally sputtered out the room was full of smoke and all the lights were out again. So I got up, put on my long johns, electric socks, insulated boots, and my heavy winter coat, and crawled back into bed and went to sleep.

At four a.m. I woke up gasping for breath. The room was humid with a foul deadly odor. I wrapped a towel around my head and ran into the kitchen. My roommate had turned on the oven and all the gas burners on the stove in an attempt to heat the place. His mistake was in leaving them on when he went to bed. During the night the flames had gone out and gas had leaked steadily till now the atmosphere of the apartment was deadly as the air on Venus and about ready to explode. It was nice and toasty warm in the kitchen though. Unfortunately, to preserve our lives I had to open all the doors and windows to air the place out. By the time I closed them, the indoor and outdoor thermometers were running neck and neck: twenty-nine degrees.

The next morning I got up to take a piss. I lifted the seat and stood there with a stream of cirrus clouds rolling from my mouth. Something was wrong. Where was the familiar tinkling sound? I looked down and saw that the water in the bowl was frozen solid as a polar lake. Someone had taken a crap on the ice and the turd sat there unimmersed, waiting for the spring thaw when it could be flushed. I turned to stomp out and slipped up on the icy floor left over from my bath the night before. My limbs became ridiculous windmills as I fell back against the cold radiator. I hit it hard. As soon as I moved my arm I knew it was broken.

Later that afternoon as I came home from the hospital with my right arm in a plaster cast I wondered what else could go wrong. As soon as I stuck my key in the front door, the entire building exploded. All my worldly possessions fell around me in flaming hunks. Oh well, at least I was finally warm.

BROTHER BOB

Brother Bob was a three hundred pound dealer known for his impeccable suits and tiny round spectacles thick as paper weights that gave him a lurid look of frog eyes. He used to eat a hit and a half of acid just to get himself out of bed in the morning. I don't remember ever seeing him when he wasn't under the influence of some drug. At Grateful Dead shows you'd often see him hovering above the crowd like a medicine ball, levitating higher than the stoned masses on ever more experimental stimulants. What he dealt and what he did varied drastically but it was always stronger than the average shit.

"No matter what our delirium we must always remember quality," he used to say. One time I ran into him at a Frost show after he'd just gotten out of jail for trafficking. He produced a small blue jar full of uncut Peruvian flake and we did mega blasters off a baby's teething spoon until my metabolism hit such a squeal that I had to dance off into the crowd.

Everybody was a brother or sister to Bob. Even Jenny Muldoon, who you'd better call MISS Muldoon, was Sister Jenny to Bob. The postman was "Brother Postman," the maid was "Sister Cleaning Woman." I heard when they busted him, Bob addressed each member of the SWAT team as "Brother Cop."

Brother Bob would do drugs that hadn't been classified or even named yet. He thought nothing of eating seven hits of acid at four a.m. If cocaine had kept him awake for five days straight he would just swallow a couple of quaaludes to calm himself down. No matter how much zip or coke he did, he never lost a pound. When he got a ring of sweat around his underarms he would change into a clean new white shirt. Brother Bob never looked disheveled or poorly dressed, even when his hands shook so much he couldn't zip up his pants. He had a closet full of suits to express the mood of whatever drug he was on.

One incident about him sticks out in my mind. At the time I was seventeen and living in crash pads around San Francisco. Brother Bob was dealing everything out of a little

Victorian near the Panhandle. When I went to visit him he was cooking tacos, six at a time in a huge iron pan. I don't know what he was on, but it was some serious upper because he was clenched over the stove, with every muscle in his body rippling and sweat just raining down off him. The tacos didn't even have a chance to make it to a plate, he ate them directly out of the pan, shoving two into his mouth at a time. When I walked in he said hello between crunches, his beady little glasses fogged over with hysterical mist.

"I don't know if you'll want to stay," he said. "I got a big deal going down in a few minutes."

"It's okay," I said, "I've seen deals go down before." But not like this.

When the doorbell rang Brother Bob slipped on a tuxedo jacket and ushered the buyer in. It was a blind man about seventy years old with two teenaged attendants. The old man was gaunt and thin, the paleness of his face further highlighted by the black glasses. He wore a tailor made Italian suit, total organized crime material. The attendants were a pair of fifteen year old blonde girls. Even though the old man was blind, he had taken great care to make sure that his seeing eye girls were quite beautiful.

After a few mumbled pleasantries Brother Bob walked into the next room and reemerged with two suitcases full of LSD. We're talking like fifty thousand hits. The old man picked up a sheet and licked it lightly. The girls commented on what pretty designs they were. Then they closed them up and the blind man walked out, each girl carrying a suitcase on either side of him. One of the girls handed Bob a backpack full of bills before he closed the door. Afterwards Bob looked up at me and asked, "So, you want any tacos?"

I was halfway through my second one when I noticed the tortilla was biting back because, yes, Bob had dosed the salsa. As the room began to melt I looked over at him with a surprised expression on my face. Brother Bob just smiled.

"That, my boy," he said, "is the taste of quality."

INCORRIGIBLE

The four of us were going to see Third World play at the Warner Theater and Sir Harv had been pounding Buds in the back seat all the way to D.C. So by the time we got out the car he had him a rock steady sway. A pissing, spitting drunk, petulant as an old fag towards all of existence, with human beings despised in particular, Sir Harv on a binge was a tornado, a Tazmanian devil that tore through people's egos as if they were flimsy stones. At the theater he cussed at everyone all the way down the aisles to our seats. Before the band even starts he's up dancing, shaking his fat old black ass like he's John Travolta. The ushers keep trying to order him back into his seat, but after fifteen minutes and twenty attempts they give up, taking him for granted as a force of nature. Around the twelfth song he's killed his wine sack and calmed down a bit. As he comes back down the aisle it's obvious he has trouble telling which of the one empty chair is his. But we don't worry. Harv's good at keeping it down.

Third World slips into a solid reggae groove and some girl in the row in front of us gets up and starts dancing. She's got a huge butt and it's in a pair of jeans tight as tattoos. All four of us start staring at it like it's a disco ball or something. There's a steady haze in the place so we fire up a big hooter. Sir Harv's just staring straight ahead but we hand it to him anyway. He takes a big lung busting hit. And starts coughing. Hack! hack! hack! He's shaking all around and his eyes are tearing as he leans forward in the chair coughing even more. Then he opens his mouth wide and projectile vomit shoots out in a thick paisley stream. All over the girl's ass. Big chunks of it are dripping off the rear pockets of her tight jeans. For a few seconds she just keeps dancing. But then she starts to feel something funny. She hesitates. It's seeping in. She stands completely still, her eyes big as a zombie's. Then she reaches gingerly back to touch her ass with her fingertips. And I thought she was going to get sick too. By this time Sir Harv had already slunk off, and it was just the three of us sitting there. She spun around and gave us a look of pure psychopathic venom. We just shrugged our shoulders, but she didn't seem too convinced of our innocence.

During the intermission I ran into Sir Harv again. He was at the bar drinking. When I demanded an explanation he smiled, toasted me, and said, "Just making room for some more."

ENRIQUE

I remember Enrique the hottest of the Latin lovers who could do the cha-cha for sixty-nine hours straight. He slept with a thousand women and loved them all. But despite his sexual conquests he always believed himself to be ugly because he had one fully developed breast like a woman's. It is said that the night he married his first wife this breast began to produce milk and he nursed his new bride between the nuptial sheets. Supposedly the milk had incredible aphrodisiac powers, one sip would send women into a frenzy and they would crawl about on all fours moaning for raw meat. All the wives from the neighboring villages would line up outside the walls of Enrique's house and beg for just a shot glass of his milk.

He would appear on a balcony impeccably dressed in a white linen suit with a hole strategically cut over the magic breast and would squeeze out a mug full which he then flung over the crowd. Instantly the women became braying animals rolling about in the mud fingering themselves. Their husbands who had been hiding in a corn field next to the scene would burst into the open and be ravaged by their horny mates in an orgy so spectacular that many of the exhausted husbands in the later stages were forced to employ corn cobs as dildoes.

Many of the children born in the baby booms after his arrival were named Enrique. Prostitutes from hundreds of miles around gave up wealthy lives to live as Enrique's chaste house servants. The best marriages which had lasted for years were broken so that the wives could throw themselves at Enrique's feet. He would allow them to live in his stable for a few days and then send them on their ways. Every night twenty virgins were waiting for him in his bedroom. His wife had to beat them off with a statuette of the Madonna. But still the hoards of women threw themselves at the bosomed man. There seemed to be some great sadness in his eye that they all wanted to cure, and indeed, he was very unhappy. And how, you may ask, can a man of a thousand delights still carry sorrow?

Enrique liked men.

A THOUSAND POINTS OF LIGHT

I knew this guy who was a Deadhead who once went to this Skinny Puppy concert with a head full of Yellow Dragon tabs. Now he was used to the mellow hippie scene, all the flower kids blissed out to Jerry so Skinny Puppy with their synthesized screams and audio samples of industrial accidents were really giving him a bad trip. When the video monitors started playing tapes of Auschwitz he bummed out totally and had to leave the club. He wandered around the empty parking lot in complete despair, lost and frightened. He kept looking over his shoulder for people who were after him.

When some cops drove by he flagged them down and begged them to save him from the bad vibes. He told the officers about the LSD and everything. They took him to a mysterious drug clinic. Though he was really spaced out for the rest of the night, he vaguely remembers being examined by some doctors who split his penis in half and then sewed it back together. I suggested to him that what they had really done was implant a tiny urine analysis device in him. Now whenever he did drugs and took a piss a tiny red light would appear on a big map of the United States at a Central Command Post.

After all, why do you think they call it a thousand points of light?

THE TIME THING

Goddamn the president starting wars everywhere killing everyone young, greasing up the prick of big business to shove up all our asses, turning the ozone into tar baby soot, piranhas and ass chewers from top to bottom, the boss bitching all day long, day in day out, all week long, week after week, year after year, one third of my life I listen to, put up with his boring useless drivel, I worked overtime this week, he wants me to come in Saturday and work double overtime so the landlord can get his rent. Bills like leeches on every waking moment, Pacific Gas and Electric wants its pound of flesh and so does the IRS, AT&T, State Tax Board, Water Department, Board of Equalization, hitting me till I'm punch drunk, and I've lied to everyone I've ever known, and taken great care to reinforce their most negative behaviors and give them what spare moments that are left after the backlog of years given to the shit that constantly revolves around me.

Life is just a cave of mouths chewing you the whole way so you gotta move faster, buy a new car before the last one was paid off, scream at the backup on the freeway, because don't these people realize that every minute has already been spoken for and they all belong to someone else? I'm running behind and by the time I catch up to one thing I'm late for three others, got ulcers, bad mental health, weird sexual deviations that everyone's sure to find out about but I don't have time to think about that now because so-and-so's waiting for me and I'm late for work again and that was supposed to be done three weeks ago, and I should be further along, everyone's passing me by, this is a race isn't it?

Do you forget the American Dream when you wake up or do you have to be asleep to see it? I don't got time to worry about it because I missed my bus and have to run, do some cocaine to speed me up, drink a lot to sleep for two hours so I can keep going, no rest for the weary, you only rest in peace, and you can't get that gravestone till it's paid for and I still owe bills from being alive, and my friends want more time, and my family wants more time, and my boss raised my hours from forty to sixty, I got thirty-six hours worth of appointments on Tuesday, fifty-two on Wednesday, and a whole month's worth on Thursday, and I don't even know where I am in this or where I'm going, but I know there will be too much to do when I get there.

What do you mean you need time for yourself? You owe me! You owe, owe, owe your boat till the paddles break and your insurance company raises your rates to buy new ones. What's going on in China? Who's killing all those people down south? Aren't we spinning into the sun? I ain't got time to worry about it cause she's breaking up with me because I don't spend enough time with her, and I gotta find a second job before rent's due, brushing my teeth with credit cards, I'm late for a wedding, funeral, and job interview that all started at the same time, breaking watches and clocks so I don't have to see how many hours I've lost, the cheese is over there, no over there, no there, behind Door # 1, 2, 3, when I get there it's always someplace else, I gotta keep running, going, no money, no time.

Yes, it's time. Time for the people who can't stand it anymore to get a gun and go shoot some people. This is the only logic that our system knows. A continual push, push, pushing well past the breaking point. It could snap any one of us. And yet we have the nerve to still wonder where our monsters come from.

BLUR

The mainstay of my diet here is alcohol. At night I cruise a delusive world of parties. People sitting in a dingy room smoking black hash before scrawling on the walls. Then in the back room boyfriend and girlfriend boiling up a vicious fight. Enraged, he slams his head through a wall. The next morning she claims the hole's in the shape of a heart. Her apartment is full of cats pouncing on moths in the black light.

Late night. Yellow walls closing in. Dingy crucifix on the wall. Too much beer. Too much pot. There is no sleep at the beach. It runs off into alleyways like the wild cats on the boardwalk. Tonight after work I walked the night walk through party talk from one funky little apartment to another. And everywhere I went people were tripping. They were wandering through the night giggling at dead starfish in the surf. And I hung out with one mohawked dude, us smoking from a chrome bong and him gabbing about his mom jet-setting between Ireland and the U.S. before taking the tree and ring from the owner of a McDonalds and settling in Lancaster, PA. I can feel the sleep moving in but I don't want to succumb. Maybe beach people fear dreams. Things are breaking into smaller pieces. I spent the whole night looking for dope for my job's employee party tomorrow night. Everybody else was supposed to bring potato salad and party favors, but beside my name it said: "Jon, we like your idea - bring it."

In the black light of the apartment of cats she caresses on her most feline makeup and stalks me among the plants before pouncing on my rat, and for a while everything is sweat, and from the salty beads emerges the memory of a girl at college, us making love like panthers in her dorm room while in the dozens of rooms around us people were sleeping on a clear spring night.

The beach is cold and windy today. The surf punks hang up their boards. A little girl who looks just like Pebbles on *The Flintstones* sits in a deep sand hole and cries. As I feel the sun's heat bleed out of my flesh, I remember last night's employee party. I'm a cook at a gourmet restaurant. The centerpiece of the apartment was a door that opened to nowhere and was decorated with art deco masks and pink surgical gloves. The short cherubic waiter kept blowing me prissy kisses. Terry the coke fiend who continually spouts schizophrenic haiku while he waits tables, was demonstrating kung fu and jujitsu moves. He grabbed an empty bong and twirled it around just like nun-chucks. Ralph the redneck, who invests his every cent in a high jacked 8000 horse power racing stripe big red machine GTO that he tirelessly cruises the Avenue in, was fascinated by a book on modern art and for two hours plunged into paintings by Picasso, Matisse, and other names he's never seen. He is fat, wears glasses, and is in love with every waitress who ever worked at the restaurant. His attempts to pick them up are incessant, but he never gets any. Rollo the Surf Punk was there with his girlfriend and rapidly degenerating into a late night alcohol fog. His words came out like paste and his girlfriend was more of a crutch than a leaning post. I could understand his condition though. A week ago his girlfriend got sun poisoning, and her lips and cheeks are blistered.

"I guess you don't make out too much," I said.

"Not only that, she's burned on the inside of her thighs too," he said.

Some trendy little new wave girl kept backing me into corners with sex written in her eyes. Her approach was subtle as a sledgehammer and she was sloppy drunk. I backed away. I want cunning and sobriety in my predators. Raw honesty just isn't enough anymore. Besides, I was there with a friend of mine from Newark. He had come down to see his grandfather who was in the hospital with a stroke.

"It was rough," he told me. "This morning he couldn't talk and didn't even recognize me. I almost lost it. I mean I know he's my grandfather, but I just couldn't stand to be near someone that sick. I wanted to be a psychologist but now I just don't know."

We got into an intense conversation about Bunuel movies that went on and on, and when we looked up the apartment was deserted except for a tubby waitress passed out on a bed, and another night had been wasted.

47

"What's your name?"

"Specimen," said the punk with a purple mohawk and iron cross earring. He kept fondling the German medals on his leather jacket.

"Wild name, you work round here?"

"At George's Lunch."

"Work today?"

"They won't let me start till my hair grows out. Fuckin' long hairs."

"Who you mean by that?"

"You know, those fucking hippie conservatives. Smoking their dope, listening to the Grateful Dead and driving their Toyotas. They hate us young people."

He kept spinning the silver nose ring in the hole above his left nostril.

"Where you live?"

"At home with my parents."

"I bet you freak 'em out."

"I did at first but they see me so often it doesn't phase them anymore. I only see them at breakfast and we don't say anything. I just munch on Pac-Man cereal and they eat Shredded Wheat and Herbalife."

"What are they like? Longhairs?"

"Yeah," said Specimen.

Whenever I go to sleep the birds are always singing and the sky's pink as an albino's eye. After nights like the one we talked around the room of Specimen caught in the men's room by the gym fucking a thermos stuffed with raw hamburger.

"Make me a burger, big boy!" I screamed.

In jokes evolve between cheap beers. Dada Trash's tales of pulling salt-water taffy on the Boardwalk, and Foul Val who screamed at him, "I bet your dick is soft like taffy."

"Yeah, but when you lay it on a table for an hour it gets real hard."

"Bet it would melt in your mouth, Val."

"Nothing melts in my mouth."

Patty said, "Some people use other people as crutches."

Pip said, "But Gonzo always uses his crutches on other people."

And I remember Lea the night eight of us tripped, hanging out on the boardwalk. She kept going on about Lance the
Boy Wonder who sounded like the eighth wonder of the world
with nine inches of American Dream, perfect for two days in a
hermetically sealed hotel room. And she hurt her ass and
mumbled something.

"What?" Eric said.

"I hurt my coccyx bones," she said.

"They don't sound very sick of cock to me."

And I remember the dawn we ran home in the rain,
how the water flooded like a river down the alley making it
look like Casablanca and the fecund darkness of an apartment where everything descended into touches.

Dada Trash told some long story about how he nick-
named this Arab guy he works with "Licorice" and he called
his son "Ahmed Licorice" which was Arabic for "Son of
Licorice."

"Well," he said, "I know it's sort of an anticlimactic
ending but..."

"Made my mind cum," I said.

And the little skate punk shredders schralp mondo
fakies on Spike's ramp. The bettys are stoked and none of
them don't. Today I saw two lesbians boogie boarding in the
surf going up and down in the cold foam. Riding, gliding a
long tube into the sand. When we were kids this was play, but
today we fling a thousand nouns on the waves and scrawl
them on walls of pizza joints and Key Largo style bars where
smooth fudgepackers smack lipstick lips and the needle on
the stereo slips from Dead Kennedys to Suicidal Tendencies to
Discharge and that thrashing slashing rawness that rises
from the slam dancers curls up like a beast and screams
louder than the sharks outside the surf.

Morning arrives too quickly or is not seen at all.

We were laying in bed afterwards.

"Do you get visions during sex?" I asked.

"No, just feelings. Do you see anything?"

"Many things. This time I saw horrible machine creatures with human personalities. They were made of alchemi-

49

cal tubing and strange pumps all in a sexual operation of pistons, sockets, and gaskets."

"That sounds horrible."

"No, it was great. Like a different world. I probably saw it cause Pink Floyd was playing. Once I saw red lizards."

"Do you always see stuff?"

"No, lots of times I just think up Fantastic Four stories. Right when I reach orgasm Galactus the World-Eater wins and the cosmos blows up. I want to name my first child Galactus. I could call him 'Gal' for short."

There's some afflicted old dude who washes dishes at the Avenue restaurant. Everyone calls him the Catman. He looks like he's been on some serious thorazine since birth. Just walks around staring with his mouth open. Feeds cats. All the time, everywhere, stray and domestic. Leaves the Safeway store every day with a red wagon full of food, and bunches of cats cluster round him cause they know what's coming. He feeds hundreds of cats, more than he can afford to feed, and the restaurants give him scraps.

I was drinking at the Front Page with a waiter from work and he tells me the Catman used to be a college professor who was in a motorcycle accident and is shellshocked. But I think he just got tired of all the shit, told the world to fuck off and is going to spend the rest of his life making cats happy.

Letter to the editor of a local paper written the day after Dada Trash was arrested for skateboarding:

```
To the Editor:

Last night a friend of mine was grabbed, verbally abused,
and had his skateboard taken from him. Who you may ask
was responsible? A group of thugs, adolescent vandals?
No, the Rehoboth Beach Police. My friend was handcuffed,
publicly embarrassed, arrested, and taken to the station.
He was not read his rights. He has no previous record,
not even a speeding ticket. What was the charge? Riding
a skateboard on the sidewalk - a law he was not even aware
existed. It was a hundred dollar board and he won't see
```

it again. Why is it that throughout the state of Delaware
the Rehoboth Beach Police are known for their belliger-
ence, rough treatment, lack of etiquette and ignorance of
proper police procedure? Since I have lived in Rehoboth,
I have seen police officers enter houses without warrants,
beat up a seventeen year old kid, insult pedestrians and
generally conduct themselves in the fashion of prison in-
mates or lower forms of primates. The general opinion
among both tourists and residents is that the Rehoboth
Police are more of a hindrance than a help and are more
concerned with collecting petty fines than in keeping the
peace. If this is true then what we have is an ugly little business and not a law enforcement agency. The image
they present to the entire state is that of a neo-Nazi
playpen for ignorant rednecks on a macho trip. If these
guys want to play Rambo why don't they go to Nicaragua?
The people and the tourists in this town deserve something
better. Just a modicum of politeness would be a nice
start. I have not included my name and address because
not only do I fear harassment, I expect it.

They didn't print the letter.

Tonight after practice Kevin invited this band called
Head Hurt back to our sleazy little dive we affectionately call
the Shithole. But it's developing character, the walls sinking
into lichens of collage and paintings of biological abstractions. The drummer was twelve years old, wore Coke bottle
glasses, had a mohawk, and complained that he didn't like
hearing people talk about philosophy before he went to sleep.
Him and this goofy looking guitarist had worked out a routine
that went:
        "My name's Chubby."
        "What?"
        "Chubby."
        "Why?"
        "Don't know."
        "How long?"
        "Since born."
        "Who?"

51

"Dad calls me Chubby. Mom calls me Chubby. Even my dog calls me Chubby."

"What's that painting of?" the little geeker asked.

"Biological abstractions," I said.

It was a glob of slimy mollusk shapes with screaming mouths on it.

"Why did you paint it?"

"It sat on my chest in a dream so I had to paint it."

"That's a good reason," hurumphed the geeker.

"Tell me more," said Kevin.

"It oozed and I fucked it," I said.

"Then you killed it and ground it up into pieces," growled Kevin.

"Put them," I crackled, "in the guacamole dip at the restaurant I work at."

"And ground the rest up and put it in the paints you painted the picture with," snarled Dada Trash.

"At night when no one's looking it still oozes and smells like a dick popped cunt," shrieked the geeker.

Then I looked over at the guitarist who had drawn a mask of a piss-in-your-pants scared face on a piece of paper, with a hole cut out for his mouth and he said, "Look, this is how I give myself head!"

"No one else will," belched Dada Trash.

The geeker bubbled, "You look like a dick smoker, Specimen."

"A what?" I asked.

"A dick smoker, a fudgepacker, you know, a homo."

"I got nothing against the gays in this town. They're the ones with all the money."

Specimen picked at his bald head and said, "Man, I heard Ronald Reagan's planning a full scale invasion of Beirut."

"Well," I sighed, "I always wanted to see another country. Where's a good place to desert to?"

"Fuck that, we'll go over there and kick their asses," snarled Kevin.

"Have fun," said Dada Trash. "Rest in pieces."

"War will be just like slam dancing."

"What about the chemical dumps in New Jersey?" said

Specimen. "Pretty soon mutants will be born in them and they'll rise up and make everything radioactive."

"You a dumb shit."

"You booking?"

"Yeah," I said. I glued a Coke can to the ceiling and walked out into the night searching for that sacred sight, beach boy's plight, a blond with a head like a fishbowl full of alcohol and sex.

One of my roommates, Kevin, has fucked two girls a day, every day since he's been here. None of them has been older than seventeen. He's twenty-three. So we don't let him fuck in the house anymore. This doesn't stop him. He takes them to the graveyard, says there's one headstone that's great for eating a girl out on.

Later in the summer when we were illegally evicted, beaten, and had all our money taken by the Rehoboth Police Department, they pulped Kevin with a billy club and charged him with assaulting a police officer. Me and John were the only ones who didn't get taken away. We didn't even get back from the party until all our roommates had been clubbed and it was all over. Two officers had been left behind to guard the house.

"Why have we been evicted?" we asked.

They wouldn't say anything. There was no warrant. There was no notice of eviction. There was no written anything. Just the bruises on my roommates. We're the invisible people, the ones who can't afford lawyers. A few feet from the officers, Specimen foraged through the underbrush for grubs and pretended to eat them.

"Is he yours?" asked one of the officers.

"A friend," John said.

Afterwards, we had no place to stay. No one would take Kevin in because the police were watching him. He sleeps in the graveyard now.

It all happened that night me and Dada Trash glued our appliances to the ceiling. The toaster, blender, a full table setting, even a bottle of Windex got stuck in a haphazard circle around the light fixture. We were tired of seeing the garbage on the floor so we glued it to the ceiling. The things you can do with Crazy Glue. Even Pip's shoes got adhered. Then we went out into the delirious blur of another night of heavy drinking.

And believe me, we had some venom to vent. The night before Kevin had invited this obnoxious punk rock band called Pus Spurt to stay at our house. As soon as they arrived they proceeded to trash the place and eat all our food. The ringleader, a vile braggart guitarist named Ooze, told us about his membership in a devil-worshipping cult called The Swine. It evolved out of a group of high school boys who hung out at these sand pits and got stoned and drunk. Soon they became quite territorial about their sand pit and would beat the shit out of any strangers who arrived on the scene. These antics developed into a weekend ritual of playing war with real b-b guns. As they got older they began to get into LSD and every Friday afternoon would drop a hit, go off in different directions into the woods around the pit and when they began to get off would hunt each other down with their guns. The rituals soon grew structures, molded themselves into the rough shape of a religion. Given a choice between God and the devil, they chose the devil. A black bible was written on notebook paper. Ooze pulled up his shirt revealing a jagged scar on his right side.

"This is my virgin breaker," he exclaimed. "I got it when I was seventeen. They burned it into me with a hot stick. When I'm twenty-one, I'll get one on the other side. But I don't think I'll get the other one. They just got into too weird stuff. Began sacrificing animals, stealing goats from farms. Then they started talking about sacrificing someone in the cult. That's where I drew the line and split. I don't go to the sand pits no more but I hear there's still funny things going on there. People find chips of bone in the wet ashes of burnt out campfires."

The strangest looking one in the band was the drummer who looked about ten but was really sixteen. He had some strange disease that had stunted his growth and he never tired of venting his sexual frustration on us. He was cloudy drunk and punctuated the evening by repeated vomitings in separate areas of the house.

Me and Dada Trash went to some be-bop party above

the Sea Side Pharmacy. The chicks who lived there were hot with tans dark as smooth mud and pert conical tits, but if they had any less brains they would have floated away. Their bedrooms were decorated with Duran Duran posters.

We were sitting around building a buzz, beer by beer, and somehow the conversation tramped into the subject of Vietnam, and believe me, it was a pretty sticky word batch.

"Some guy I know in Dover went," said this dude Dave. "He said that after a while in the jungles you just went crazy. The deeper you went into the green, everything just stripped away, and soon you were paranoid as hell, shooting at birds and trees, even people on your own side. One day he was out on patrol with his best friend, and his friend stepped on a land mine right in front of him, and was blown to bits. A piece of his friend hit him in the head and knocked him into a coma for three months. He said it didn't freak him out or anything and he never went schizo like the other vets. Now he sells trailers in Dover."

"I used to work with a vet on the graveyard shift at a Safeway grocery store in New Jersey," Pip bubbled. "He was a fucking freak. He used to fuck sheep. Had a coffee table in his living room with four holes drilled in it that he could put their legs into. 'Kept them right in position,' he used to say. 'Tons better than a woman. You just fuck them till they die and then throw 'em in the oven.' He insisted that cows gave the best blowjobs. He was really mellow. Some nights he'd never say a word. But every morning at six a.m. when the Hostess Twinkie man would deliver his cakes, he'd follow him up and down the aisles yelling and screaming at him, degrading him to the point of no return, calling him the most horrible names. He didn't even know the guy. The Hostess Twinkie man bore it all in complete silence, stocked his shelves and left every day without ever saying a word. Ron would follow him out to his truck, still screaming at him, calling him slime and verbally attacking his entire genealogy. He'd keep yelling at the truck till it disappeared from sight and then he'd be silent till we got off at eight. I'd try to talk to him but most of the time he'd be off in his own world.

The worst thing happened one night when we were getting stoned behind the store. In front of us was miles of marshes. Ron began staring into the grass. It had rained heavily the night before and the marshes were flooded. The full moon reflected the blades of grass on the smooth surface of the water. Ron kept staring at these reflections for almost five minutes. I kept asking him questions but he was gone. He was back there. Back in the rice paddies. He let out a long scream and began running around frantically, shaking his hands like a machine gun. I had to tackle him to get him to stop and he collapsed, put his head against my chest and cried like a baby mumbling some Oriental-sounding name. It took me about an hour to calm him down. It was pretty hairy."

"Wild," I said. "My boss at work told me about a friend of his who went to Vietnam in '68. The guy was fresh out of the University of Alabama with a degree in engineering and ready to start on a highly paid upwardly mobile career when bam! He gets drafted. The army came to him and said, 'Look, you're intelligent, you have a degree, we'll make you an officer and you'll see very little or no front line action.' But he turned them down and went in as a private because enlisted men served only two years whereas officers were in for four. He didn't mind serving his country, but he wanted to go in, get it over with, and go on with his life. Every month while he was in, the army came to him and asked him if he wanted to be an officer and every month he turned them down; he just wanted to get his tour of duty over with. After every one of these refusals, he was demoted or sent to a worse position. Pretty soon he was on the front lines in the harshest areas of fighting. Half the nights on the line he was woken by napalm.

Two months before his two years were over, the army came to him again and asked if he wanted to be an officer. He refused yet again. They demoted him to battalion spotter. What a battalion spotter did was when a fighting group was about to invade an area, they would send about ten men out ahead into the jungles with walkie talkies to radio back whether they had drawn enemy fire or stepped on any land mines. It had the highest mortality rate of any position in the army. In order to save his life this guy went to the Vietnamese black market and paid two thousand dollars for an injection of malaria and had some old man shoot him up. In two days he was deathly ill, and in less than a week he was on a medical transport to Hawaii, then the States. Now fifteen years later he still has to take medication for the malaria, but my boss says he's never regretted his decision."

"Man, this conversation is getting pretty beat. What're we going to talk about next? Amputations? Dead babies? Let's pick it up. Talk about reefer, fucking chicks or bad surf movies."

"Tan Brownie's ex-lover came from a bad movie."

"Who's that?"

"Let me tell this tale," begged John and waited till everyone's attention focused firmly on him, bathed in the glow, swelled up his chest like a cobra about to spit, his face self-satisfied, powerful, volatile.

"Tan Brownie," he bit, "is this flaming homosexual who's our realtor. For about two weeks he's been trying to pass off his ex-lover as a roommate for his tenants. His ex-lover is hideous. The guy's a scruffy scungy greaseball who talks infrequently and only in non sequiturs, has never bathed, and hides his face beneath a perpetual mold of two-day beard growth. He owns only one outfit of clothes: black disco pumps, unmatched socks, green polyester pants, and a Hawaiian shirt. He hasn't washed it or taken it off in the two weeks we've known him. At parties he mumbles to himself and occasionally talks to the walls or house plants. As a roommate, no one has been able to put up with him for more than two days because of his penchants for seeing large furry creatures that just plain aren't there.

He stayed with this girl we know for one night and she kicked him out in the morning. About six times during the night he crept into her room, woke her up and said, "It's out in the kitchen!"

"What?"

"The creature!"

"Oh, you mean the cat."

"No, not the cat. The other thing. The big hairy thing."

He wouldn't let her sleep till she went out and checked. Every time it was just the cat. This dude's a real freak."

"Not as freaky as Candy and Shannon," I said. My roommates let out a moan. Candy Cane and Shannon were two drag queens one of my roommates had brought home from a gay bar called the Crystal Closet. Candy looked like a long-haired heavy metal redneck in red fuck-me pumps, panty hose, and a gold lame body suit bulged out up top with 100 percent cotton falsies. He had hairy legs. Hearing his harsh voice in those Frederick's of Hollywood clothes made the hair on your scalp do an electric war dance.

Shannon was actually very pretty as a girl, except that he was six and a half feet tall. He wore a conservative floral blouse and a lavender skirt. His voice was soft and his manners petite, strange in a physique so monolithic. Candy was the bigger queen. He claimed he was moving to Ireland in the fall so he could get a sex change for free on welfare. "I was born in little boy's pants, but I don't plan on dying in them!" he shrieked. As soon as they arrived they began trying to rape all my male roommates.

"I know I'm going to sleep with two of you," moaned Candy, "and only one of you is sitting down."

Everyone looked around the room. Kevin was the only one standing. He's depressingly heterosexual. Kevin blushed so red I thought he'd reached critical mass.

"No thanks," he said. "I have a headache."

"I got a headache too," retorted Candy, "I got an ache in my dick head."

"Now Blanche," said Shannon, "act like you have some manners. These people were nice enough to bring us to their garage apartment and all you want to do is sit on the first thing that pops up."

"Baby, don't I! This butt can take up anything. It just gobbles it up. I've taken up to twelve inches up it, anything longer would just be gone, you'd never see it again. It'd be the lost object."

"Blanche, all you want to do is nookie. I couldn't keep you off the laps of every underage boy in the Crystal Closet."

"I want to go swimmin'. Any of you boys want to go to the beach? I'll go down there, rip my bra off, throw my fake titties on the sand and say, 'Here they are boys. Suck em!' Come on, none of you all have lived till you've had a real sissy."

We all turned him down. So we just sat around for a couple hours drinking a lot of rum and listening to them lisp on. Then Dada Trash came up with an idea. Two lifeguards lived in the house in front of us. They were your typical stereotypical Rehoboth Beach lifeguards: chauvinistic, cute, muscular, tanned, alcohol abusers, homophobic, conservative, dumb, preppy. They only slept with blondes and one called all women "bettys." They were passed out from drinking too much and now were easy fodder for our plan.

"We know two guys you have to meet," said Dada Trash. "And we may even get you all laid."

He led Candy and Shannon into the front house and into the lifeguards' room. We roused them up to a half-drunken half-woken stupor and said, "Man, we got two bettys here. They've heard all about you two. They're really drunk and they want to fuck you."

"Cool!" said one as he jumped out of bed, and both of them dove into pickup conversation with all of their macho gusto. But slowly over the next five minutes of talk in the darkened room they began to realize that these weren't girls. A sick look slowly grew across their faces and you could actually see their pallors whiten. One looked as if he had been drop kicked in the testicles. He looked around frightened as if he could not understand how he had woken up in this strange place with these two sex-crazed men pretending to be women. Then he realized he lived there. The look pasted to his face was priceless. We rolled.

"Get 'em out of here," he begged. "Get 'em out!"

The other lifeguard kept trying to hide under the covers but we kept pulling the sheets off his face. When Candy and Shannon finally left, the lifeguards made us lock them into the room.

But it only took Candy and Shannon a few minutes to find new prey. Asleep on the front porch was a fifteen year old skate punk who had materialized out of nowhere. He had hitchhiked down from New Jersey two days before, knew no one in the house, was probably a runaway, and yet had somehow managed to flim flam his way into living there without paying rent. Candy and Shannon goosed him awake and chased him into the kitchen where me and Pip's girlfriend were sitting at the table. The skate punk looked at us as if he didn't know whether to feel frightened or virile.

"Do you know what a transvestite is?" Candy barked at the kid.

"No."

"It's a man who not only dresses like a woman but wants to be one as well."

The kid's face squished. They'd crushed his reality.

"You mean you two ain't girls?" he stammered.

"Thank you sugar, that's the best compliment I've gotten all night."

The skate punk ran out of the room. Candy ran after him screaming, "When I get my pussy this fall I'm going to come back here and fuck little fifteen year old boys like you!" Shannon brought up the rear. The transvestites chased him off into the night and we never saw the kid again.

Two days later I saw Candy and Shannon on the boardwalk. Shannon was wearing a leopard skin one piece swim suit. Candy was wearing skin tight white shorts, a crimson scarf, falsies, and a cut off t-shirt that said "It's tough being a sex symbol." They were cruising for surfer boys and wouldn't tell me what happened to the skate punk. Maybe he had become the lost object.

I saw Candy and Shannon only one more time. It was at four a.m. on the boardwalk and they were dressed as men. They looked much stranger as men than as drag queens. Late at night the real freaks prowl the boards in search of wordless guilt-saturated fucks. Candy and Shannon were so giddy and harmless that this dark scene seemed too cold for them. They walked past stiffly, uncomfortable in their masculine personas, like young children in starched Sunday clothes. They walked past without even recognizing my presence and disappeared into the distance of benches, boards, and discarded popcorn, two strange sexual ghosts swallowed by the four a.m. delirium.

For a few minutes I just let my mind phase out of the conversation and drift like a gull over all the shit that had been going down at our place. Dada Trash was living in sin in the back room with a seventeen year old runaway. That morning Specimen had run into our apartment wearing only a towel. Specimen had two thin lines of hair on his head that he had rubber cemented so they stood straight up, and they were spray painted florescent red. "Look," he said, "I have to show this to someone." He opened the towel to reveal a used cum-and-poontang-coated half-off rubber drooling from his dick like a snake skin.

"I just lost my virginity," he exclaimed. "I'm not going to take it off for a week."

When I came back to the conversation they were talking about life.

"I only see life through a bong," belched Dave. I laughed so hard I almost shit.

"Man, I know this guy," continued Dave, "who was eating this girl's pussy and she pussy farted all over his face, man. I mean brap! And whoosh, his hair was all blown back, there was this big green cloud around his head."

"Crabs dripping from his ears!"

"Like one second he's thinking fish and the next second he's thinking dog shit!"

"Yes, but did she have big tits?"

"Man, tits are beautiful, but pussy's much more practical."

"Yesterday we saw this black kid walking down the middle of the Avenue in heavy traffic with a white pillow case over his head, made him look like a KKK klansman, in the middle of heavy traffic, and there were no eye holes cut in the pillow case."

"Sometimes I just think it's the end of the world."

The beer had chewed us to exhaustion, its teeth savage, but our struggle with it was unrelenting, even though many of us had to be at work in a couple hours. Eyes halfmast, liquid blue in stupor. The smell of marijuana had become a new layer of skin, soiled itchy feel of clothes worn too long, weak cells screaming for a shower, sleep no longer an option but an accident. Soon the orange sky would burst atomic from the sea. But this was that longest dark before dawn. The unraveled hour. Where the longest lines of cocaine lay. But we were poor, drunk, with minds like sour turds waiting to be flushed. At that very moment, my roommate Kevin was probably fucking a fourteen year old girl in the graveyard.

It was the grey light before dawn. Dada Trash and I

stumbled home, the only things moving in a paralyzed landscape. Even the police were still asleep. The whole world was about to awake, rise from its cocoon of night with new life, but we were too dead to notice. We were running down like a cheap watch you'd buy on the boardwalk. Three things were on our minds: Eat, Piss, Sleep. Painful blocks of walking. Then home. Tan Brownie's ex-lover was passed out on the front steps and the punks from Pus Spurt were spraying him with solvent and lighting him on fire.

PAYBACKS ARE A BITCH

Three years ago a drunk passed out on our front porch and Specimen set him on fire. That was then. This happened later. It was a Saturday night and there was nothing going on. Around eleven o'clock I got a call from Ed that they had a couple cases of beer and were jamming at the Slip House. Just as I was about ready to go, Specimen showed up with a couple other skinheads in tow. He promptly passed out on our living room floor. I kicked him awake and managed to get him out the front door. So he passed out on the front lawn. The grass was soaked with dew and rain but he didn't care. Me and the skinheads kicked him awake again, got him on to his feet, and kept him moving.

The Freudian Slip House was your typical bohemian crash pad. In its rooms paintings and black light posters hung above a chaos of empty beer cans, overflowing ashtrays, and dirty bongs. As we walked toward the house Will Enticer was doing nude pushups on the center line of Cleveland Ave. Suddenly, as headlights began to bear down on him from both directions he hopped up and ran toward the curb. Since his pants were down around his ankles he hobbled along with tiny baby steps. Will Enticer was the lead singer of The Freudian Slips and the ultimate rock and roll animal. He wasn't a very good singer or guitarist, but he sure knew how to live the lifestyle. Alcohol was his oxygen and pussy the basis of his diet. At parties he had a tendency to jump up on kitchen tables, take off his clothes, and play bad seventies pop songs on the acoustic guitar. If he was ever castrated half the women in Newark would go into mourning.

Me and the skinheads went in and started drinking beer. Specimen passed out on the couch in the living room. All the regulars were there and pretty soon we started a pickup jam in the basement. Hot blues and rock and roll with a seven piece band, and we were cooking up some mean sounds. The songs grew into each other like living things while the beer flowed down easy. While we were throbbing the basement, Will jumped off the roof in the nude. Luckily he landed in a bush and was only badly bruised. All the alcohol in him kept away the pain. After about an hour and a half the neighbors started banging on the walls, and the tunes were sloshing into double vision anyway, so we called it quits and went up to the front porch to cool off. We were all wet with that good sweat you get after a bout of creativity, with your fingers tired from strumming the strings and your voice hoarse from singing.

On the porch we drank more beer. Enticer kept bumming about Specimen being passed out on his couch. We didn't see what his problem was. Everyone there had Specimen pass out in their apartment dozens of times. But Enticer kept getting upset about it. He'd let the issue lie for a couple of minutes, but he kept bringing it up. More people kept showing up with more beer. Suddenly it was a real party. Will kept bumming about Specimen, even as he was playing the host.

About a half hour later I was having a conversation about Hell outside on the porch when Billy burst out the front door and yelled, "Hey people, Enticer is setting that dude in the living room on fire!"

We looked down the hallway and saw an orange glow issuing from the den. As one body we all got up and ran inside. By the time we got to the living room Specimen's body was engulfed in flames. And we're talking like stunt man flames. He was burning from the knees to the shoulders and the tongues were three feet long. Four or five people were beating him out, but since Enticer had soaked him down with lighter fluid, as soon as they put out the flames they just reignited.

Specimen woke up out of unconsciousness screaming. Finally we extinguished him and he immediately passed back out. His clothes were pretty bad off but his skin looked okay, except for a couple of big blisters on his chin.

Afterwards, we bummed on Enticer heavily. "Enticer, that was a really assholish thing to do."

"Will, you don't just set people on fire."

"How would you like it if someone did that to you?"

"What an asshole."

"I can't believe you set him on fire."

Enticer was all fucked up and just stood there sheepishly saying, "It was cool. It was cool."

"Enticer," I said, "three years ago that kid set someone on fire at our old house. Paybacks are a bitch but now he's come full circle. I'd just watch your ass in a couple of years."

At this point we stood around the kitchen talking and talking, drinking and drinking. Enticer kept justifying his actions but there wasn't much he could say. He was just plain shitfaced.

There was a constant bad karma that flowed between Will and Billy and this whole incident had really brought it to a head. Will's burning seemed to justify Billy's negative opinion of him. While Will was all wrapped up in a drunken conversation, Billy began soaking down the leg of his jeans with lighter fluid. Suddenly Will burst into flames. It looked like he had a campfire stuck on his belly. Everyone in the room began throwing beer on him. Suds went everywhere. By the time we put him out, everything and everyone in the kitchen was soaked and dripping beer. Paybacks are a bitch.

The crowd had slowly grown and soaked up more alcohol until it could no longer stand the vertigo of the house and went spilling out onto the street. Over a hundred and fifty people flowed through the downstairs, but the cool people had withdrawn to one of the small attic rooms to do some hard drugs. The room was gray and claustrophobic, with punk artwork all over the walls. By the top of the stairs up to there, was a wall hanging made of dozens of pieces of broken mirrors glued onto the paneling. We pulled off one of the shards of reflecting glass and began to cut up lines on it. Some fat girl kept turning me on to blow. Just when I got the full coke rush and waves of paranoia flowed over me in twitching gusts, the window began to flicker red and blue. Pigs. We hid our drugs, turned out the lights, and got real quiet. The cops walked into the living room and ordered everyone out of the house. Will went down to talk to them. It turned out the neighbors had complained, imagine that. After about a half hour they had cleared out everyone in the house except for those of us up in the attic room. As soon as the cruisers pulled away we broke out our drugs and started partying again.

Around this time Rich 'Bitch' Malone walked in. Rich was a local asshole. He'd been the lead singer of about four or five hardcore bands and felt he needed to live the part. This meant he had to regularly commit random acts of violence, vandalism, and personal injury. Unfortunately, the only people he ever inflicted these acts on were his friends. If he ever did them to his enemies they would have simply killed him in short order and saved us all a lot of trouble.

Close on his heels was Al Duval and his girlfriend. Al showed up with fifty dollars worth of liquor, a trash can, lemons, limes, and fifteen packs of Kool Aid and whiskey sour mix. After ten minutes of alchemy, we had five and a half gallons of iced teas. We drank round after round, smoked more pot, did more lines, and Rich started to get obnoxious. He began to insult everyone in the room, even the people he didn't know. On and on he went, ridiculing everyone around him, telling them they were shit and not "hardcore" enough to hang out with him. For an hour he went on with this steady negative monologue and all of us were just too polite to get up and beat the living crap out of him.

Rich sat there demanding bong hits and lines, badgering people till they gave them to him just to get him off their backs, then he stood up and walked around pretending he was a lot drunker than he really was, stumbling into things, knocking records and books off tables, breaking knickknacks, drooling into people's hair just to prove he was the undisputed King of the Jerks. Finally, around four a.m., he started to pass out. But then his eyes snapped open and he tried to get up to leave. Don't ask me how, but somehow his feet slipped out from under him and as he was falling he grabbed the trash can of iced teas, lifted it off the floor, and spilled four and a half gallons of liquor.

It went everywhere. Lemon wedges were sloshing against the walls. It was an inch deep on the floor and it began to rain alcohol through the ceiling of the room below. Al jumped up and grabbed Rich by the shirt, "You motherfucker!" he screamed. "That was fifty dollars worth of liquor you just spilled! Half my paycheck is on the floor now!"

Rich got a frightened look on his face and started trying to butt fuck Al. He forced Al over and started slamming his groin into Al's rear end.

"What the fuck are you doing?!" screamed Al.

"I'm trying to impregnate you!" yelled Rich.

Al's girlfriend was sitting there not knowing what to do. Should she laugh along, get embarrassed, feel jealous? As Rich stood there slamming into Al's behind, he began insulting everyone in the room. Instead of apologizing, he tried to asshole his way out of it. Al's girlfriend couldn't take anymore and walked out. Rich followed her. She began to go downstairs.

In the darkness by the top of the steps, Rich stared down at her. Then his face split in a sinister smile and he reached over to the wall hanging of mirrors and pulled off one of the longest, sharpest shards. He threw it at her head with all his might. It stabbed the flower out of her hair but luckily missed the skin. Al, who had come looking for her, jumped on Rich. They slugged it out until Rich grabbed another piece of glass from the wall and threatened him away. Al and his girlfriend ran into the attic screaming .

"Rich threw a piece of glass at me!"

"And he tried to stab me!"

"And now he's running around downstairs with a chunk of glass the size of a butcher knife, just looking for someone to cut !"

Instant pandemonium. "Oh my God ! He's finally gone over the edge!"

"He's a psychopath!"

"We should have seen this coming."

"He'll kill us all."

"Somebody's got to go down and catch him."

"Not me."

"Not me."

"Me neither."

"Well, we can't just stay here."

"Why not?"

"Call the cops."

"They were already here."

"Maybe they'll come back."

"The phone's downstairs anyway."

"We got to try and get to the phone."

"Oh no we don't."

"He'll kill us all."

Will jumped up to lock the door and knocked over the lamp. The room plunged into utter darkness. That darkness was full of screams. People were jumping under tables, hiding behind bookshelves and stacks of records, screaming, cussing, and scared shitless. "He'll kill us all!"

Finally, after a couple minutes of marrow tingling terror, we found a new bulb and screwed it into the lamp. A sigh of relief filled the room with the light. The five biggest guys banded together and walked down the stairs. The house was silent and unmoving. We kicked open doors, jumped into the dark bedrooms swinging at empty air, punched out shadows that turned out to be dressers, flicked on the light - and found nothing but an empty room. Room by terrifying room, we checked the entire house, even the closets. Rich was nowhere. He had faded like a phantom into the night. Outside the sun was coming up and there was no sight of him on the street. The next day when we had slept it all off, and woke with hangovers and obliterated memories around dinner time, many of us wondered if he had ever really been there at all.

All eighty-six people at the party got quiet to hear Eve, alone on the table, pussy fart. It's called Queebing and takes years of practice. I think she should learn to play the flute. Of course everyone assumed she was a slut, but Eve hadn't had sex since mid-summer. "The only thing that gets me off is knowing that men masturbate over me," she once said.

Dada Trash was lamenting about a lost love to me. We also called him Anti-Leonardo because of his belief that the true masterpiece will be found in a junkyard. Flea markets were his favorite hangouts.

"My life is a shambles," he said. "She was perfect. Great body, and a Christian too. Her clothes are from K-Mart but they're the most expensive brands they have. You wouldn't catch her at a Blue Light Special. Sil told me she was the holy side of my madonna/whore complex, but you know how full of shit he is. What we had was real."

"What did it this time?"

"I couldn't take it anymore. She's so unresponsive. After six months of dating she's only let me play with her tits once. I talk all the time and she just sits there and listens or ignores me, serene as a piece of lawn sculpture. It's like I'm pouring my heart in the sea. Last week I gave her a photocopy of my face and she wouldn't hang it on her wall. That's when I knew it was over."

"I heard about that. Sil was with you at the copier machines in the bank and as soon as you stuck your head under the rubber flap, Sil started screaming, 'Look everybody! This asshole's got his head stuck in a xerox machine!'"

"Man, I don't know what I'm gonna do. Should I go to Louisiana or Ocean City? I can't stay here. I've always wanted to live at the beach with an old divorcee. She'd have to be overweight and her tits don't need to be big but they have to be saggy. Most of all she needs that forty year old flesh.

"Gets you off, huh?"

"Believe me, man, there's nothing that compares, I want to fuck her upstairs while her kids are making so much noise downstairs that she has to yell, 'Shut the fuck up!' Did I show you what I got at Nemer's flea market today?"

He handed me a stack of snapshots, all depicting a dead grandmother at her funeral.

"Only cost me fifty cents."

"Nudes for a dollar," I quipped.

"I heard about you and Jill."

"Yeah...."

"It sucks, man."

"Fuck it, man, let's not talk about it. You think you'll go back with - Hey! What about that tour group at the zoo today? Those parents' faces when we dove on all fours, baaa-ed like sheep and ate grass. Ohhh shit, Chaos!"

Chaos slid toward me through the crowd. Talking with Chaos is like listening to a whirling cluster of hallucinations. He's ofttimes senseless but always overflowing with pyrotechnics. To him, beauty would be the extinction of the universe. He put a cigarette out on his tongue and went into one of his usual rants.

"I'm going to get my emotions amputated. Isn't there some surgery that can just burn out certain areas of your brain?"

"You'd look good with a lobotomy. Why, man?"

"Because thanks to a couple of close relationships this year, I can only fuck people I'm emotionally involved with. That makes me a social cripple. Nobody really loves anymore, they just play games. You can't escape it, it's the march of the computer age. We're becoming sexually compatible robots and in twenty years the only thing erotic will be the sensation of metal on flesh."

"Why, how nihilistic of you."

"Hey, I don't want to burn out all my emotions. I'll keep hate. You need that to survive."

"Fuck that, man you need some experiences, even though love is the worst thing you can do to your sanity."

"Why? It's a hari-kari feeling anyway. Love is a wound. When you're young it gets fresh lancings and the sensation levels increase until scar tissue eclipses it and you become bitter. By the time you're sixty, you just eat food."

I figured I'd shut up and take in Sil and Inga for awhile. They'd gone out for two years, busted each other's cherries. Sadistic inertia had preserved the relationship. Inga's hobby was developing emotional tortures for Sil. One night me, Dada Trash, and them were walking to a party out in Chapmoss Apartments. We were in front of the Royal Deck Pub when Inga took off through the parking lot and behind the building.

"Must have to take a piss," Sil said. We kept walking. She rejoined us on the other side of the Pub. Boy, was she mad.

"Why didn't you run after me, Sil? You don't know what could have happened behind there. I could have been raped!"

Dada Trash and I eased on ahead of them and let her go at him. Inga screamed at him all the way to Chapmoss. Sil loved it. "Humiliation is the only pure emotion," he used to say.

But now all that's changed. Inga dumped Sil for some Brazilian stud she met at Rehoboth Beach. His family's big in lumber, and owns five houses in various resort spots around the planet. We called him Panama Red. After the breakup Sil ate twenty aspirin and three speeders. Inga wasn't impressed. The next night her roommate caught her crying in the bathroom.

When I asked Inga about Panama, she said, "He's rich, he's cute, I want to marry him." Her and Panama never exchanged more than twenty-five words of conversation with each other. Inga still visited Sil and would insult him for hours.

Tonight was no exception. She was hanging on Panama and every three minutes would suck his face for thirty seconds. The rest of the time she insulted Sil. Inga started with the basics like how small his penis was and moved on to heavier subjects. Sil talked her into piercing his left nipple the following Saturday. Soon she was screaming, "Bleed for me Sil! Bleed for me!" Jill, my ex-girlfriend, had been like that, too.

I had been drinking for a long time, but it wasn't working. I sat on the couch and tried to think about nothing, like turning a TV to static. Neese gave me a few bong hits but they didn't help either. For an hour I didn't talk to anyone. Then I got up and left.

On the way home, trees glistened with ice. The savage

freakwave hit. It started deep inside and clawed up through my guts. I don't know where those swirls came from but they hurt. I thought my tears would freeze.

That night I dreamed of a girl I once loved. I'll never have her again. Sleep is the hardest time.

MOVEMENT

Gail and Kris picked me up and we went to Karl's place and Kris fucked Karl and that shouldn't have bothered me because I had slept with him too and even though me and Kris had gone out for a year, it was over and I knew that, felt that, but when they were in the other room I couldn't help feeling a horrible sense of betrayal and I went out into the twenty degree night and walked all the way across town in the wind.

Near my dorm Gail and Kris picked me up and drove me the rest of the way. It was a small car so Gail had to sit on my lap and she bounced happy, carefree, so sexual, but I thought, "I went out with her too, she's a lesbian now, stop thinking like this, you can't own things, you can't own people, even for a little while."

Our coats kept us from moving. Outside my dorm we sat and talked. They were happy. I hated Kris. I pushed something evil across the car toward her. I didn't say a word, just stared at the black outside the windshield. I couldn't move, Gail's body held down my arms and legs, I had to get out, felt like something shriveling, nauseous, paralyzed.

"I have to go," I said, and walked into the dorm without looking back. I sat in my room for five minutes, then I went out and looked through the thin window in the back door. The car was still there. Didn't they understand? Couldn't they feel me? In a few minutes, Gail said goodbye, walked into her dorm, the car drove away. For another five minutes I stood there staring at where it had been, waiting for it to come back. I knew it wouldn't.

I went back to my room and began looking around for something to break but I liked everything too much or it would have cost too much to replace and this was silly, what would it solve, it was just a waste, how could I let her make me do this? I couldn't find anything of my own that I wanted to break so I began walking around the dorm looking for a nice fragile generic piece of public property to destroy. But everything was too solid and would really hurt if I hit it and this was stupid, only drunks acted like this, why did I want to fuck myself up? I went back to my room sat on the bed and could do nothing.

But it had to go, it was too late and I began to twitch and spasm and finally jumped up and began punching the concrete wall, the hardest fucking thing in the building. And I kept punching until two knuckles were strange flat areas.

The noise woke my neighbor, Betsy. I'd just been getting to know her, she came in, bandaged my hands, and for an hour we really talked. When she left, I felt so happy. And I thought I'd probably sleep with her. The next night I did.

Steve was telling me about some guy he used to buy dope from at Yale. The dude was an expert on poisonous snakes and had an aquarium of cobras, coral snakes, or whatever venomous serpent he was studying behind his bed in his dorm room.

"It was wild," Steve said. "Here he'd turn you on to some boo-koo sinse and you'd get sort of paranoid you know, and then he'd pull out a couple of king cobras and let them crawl around the room in front of you. One of them would get close to us and we'd be screamin' and climbin' up on our chairs, but he'd be real cool and take another hit of a joint and thwack! pin it's skull with a snake pole and throw it back in the aquarium."

Supposedly he smuggled great drugs back into the States during his field trips to places like Africa and India. He hid the stash in his biological specimens. At customs the officials would take one look at skinned snakes in formaldehyde, turn up their noses, almost puke, and pass him on through.

The snake expert knew some guy who worked at the New York City morgue who was about four feet tall and five feet wide. His wife was about six feet tall and weighed eighty-five pounds. They wore all black clothing and were really into silver and turquoise spider and scorpion jewelry. Steve said they looked just like Boris and Natasha in the old Bullwinkle cartoons. They were experts on scorpions and would take field trips to South America where villagers would clear the streets when they walked into a mountain village.

The guy told the snake expert he could get him anything he wanted from the NYC morgue. How about a human body? He might even be able to come up with a big glass tank of formaldehyde to store it in. It'd make a great dorm room decoration. He could use it as a coffee table. If not a body, how about just a limb, a head or a human brain? In the end, the snake expert just ended up taking two hitchhiker's thumbs that he put on the ends of his stereo.

THE BALLAD OF HARD LUCK CHUCK

It was a sweltering summer morning when flies flew through the holes in the screens and sucked saliva off my sleeping lips that I met Hard Luck Chuck for the first time. He was passed out on the floor beside my bed. I had never seen him before. This was not a rare occurrence. I shared a two bedroom apartment with seven other people and we had been drinking for forty-two days. The bathroom and girls' room was always full of strangers. This was Rehoboth Beach and the entire population acted like this every summer. We paid an exorbitant rate for our share of the delirium.

Chuck Hotchkins had one of those faces that demanded abuse. If you connected the dot to dot acne on his face it would spell "Loser." He wasn't bad looking, with a fair body, but there was this infuriating trustfulness in him; an insecurity that vibrated at the center of his speech like a bug on a still pond; he left every conversation having made a bad impression. There was no self esteem in him. He entered every pick-up attempt knowing the girl would hate him, and with that attitude, how could she do anything but? On his second night at our house Liz had her boyfriend beat him up just for the hell of it. And in a weird way Chuck had asked for it. Don't get me wrong, there was nothing annoying or hateful about him. He wasn't arrogant or obnoxious. On the contrary, he was a beautiful trusting soul. A good guileless human being. Which is why people hated him. The man just had no defenses. Easy prey.

We called the apartment "The Flophouse For The Financially Desperate." Most of us were college students trying to save money for school. None of us saved a penny. The rest were just transients, there for the show. And what a show the summer was. An epic comedy called "Gone With My Liver," starring alcohol and LSD, with a cast of unknown sex fiends. There was a party at the Flophouse twenty-four hours a day and you only slept when the alcohol left no choice. Chuck just wandered into this.

He had quit college halfway through his senior year. A self-proclaimed 'Prisoner of Rock and Roll', he trashed academia for some glitzy dream of stardom. When you asked for details he was always vague. He couldn't play an instrument. He couldn't sing. He couldn't promote. But there was a stage waiting for him somewhere. He did know his rock and roll history though, and for his first week at the beach managed to stay drunk by winning free drinks in the bar deejays' trivia contests.

Chuck became the ninth roommate at the Flophouse and got a job at T-Shirt Factory. Around this time Sam wandered into the picture. I walked into our living room one afternoon and he was sitting in the easy chair smoking a big bone of Maui Wowie. Full head of blond hair, bushy uncombed beard and moustache, he looked like the fourth Freak Brother. Sam was a small time hustler. His favorite scam was to tell some tourists he could get them drugs, get the money fronted to him, and then run off with it. Occasionally he dabbled in petty thievery, stealing clothes, trinkets, and small cash from the local souvenir shops. Supposedly he had a grand theft auto charge drifting around Pennsylvania somewhere.

Chuck made the mistake of loaning Sam his car to go get a quarter gram of coke. Sam disappeared for two days and wrecked the car in the dunes by Ocean City. Now he sat in our easy chair smoking Maui Wowie, without Chuck's coke. When Chuck came in Sam gave him some sob story about how the dealer had ripped him off but I'd heard that line before. Chuck didn't get upset or pitch a bitch. Later I pulled him aside and said, "Man, Chuck, what are you fucking with scum like that for?"

"That's not true," said Chuck. "Everybody says that about Sam but they're all wrong. He's really a nice guy with true good in him. I'll get that money back from him." Then he went out and paid the hundred dollar repair bill on his car.

Chuck had gotten a date with a piece. And a pretty piece she was. A Jersey girl decked out in Mom and Dad's clothes, long frizzy black hair, haughty disposition, long red nails. Chuck brought her into our scum pit of a residence and dutifully fed her White Russians. He was reciting her some of his poetry when Sam walked in and started making fun of Chuck's delivery.

"Her yielding cloud accepted the bulbous yet tapered

rose of his throbbing virulenity," squeaked Sam in a high falsetto. Chuck turned red as a rose, but he offered Sam a drink anyway. The three of them sat around and talked about music. Was Springsteen God? Was Throbbing Gristle just the Sex Pistols in disguise? And what about Naomi? But after a few minutes Sam managed to steer the conversation around to his favorite subject: what a wimpy pandering useless excuse for a life Chuck Hotchkins led. The girl found it all quite funny. The White Russians had loosened her up and she laughed out loud with a horsey whine even though she sensed it hurt Chuck's feelings.

Sam kept guzzling down Chuck's hootch and laying the sly eye on the girl. She ate that twinkle right up. At one point in the conversation she leaned over and ran her fingers through Sam's beard. He wouldn't let up. He told her that Chuck used to always come to him for advice because Chuck couldn't get it up.

"I don't understand it," Sam said. "How'd Chuck get a date with a girl like you? He usually only goes out with ugly chicks. And I mean real dogs. You must weigh a hundred pounds less than his last date."

She neighed. But what a bod. Every time she laughed her big breasts heaved out like a changing of the tides.

"One time," Sam cried, "he was so hard up he went out with a girl who only had one leg!" Chuck just sat there and fidgeted. He would always tell me that no matter what, he wouldn't sink to Sam's level.

Sam and the girl kept moving closer together, occasionally his hand would fall onto her leg. They drank up all Chuck's booze, and sent him out to get more. He, of course, obeyed. When he got back from the liquor store, they were gone. Chuck shrieked in rage and picked up the vodka bottle, ready to throw it against the wall, but he caught himself at the last second, realizing this was just a waste of good alcohol and yet another thing lost to Sam.

When I walked in the door he had finished half the bottle. "Let's go to Ocean City!" he shouted.

"Okay."

When we got on the Coastal Highway, Chuck began driving 110 miles per hour. He was already tipsy. "Don't you think you're going a little fast, Chuck?" I advised.

"Weekend! Weekend!" he screamed. It was Wednesday night.

We drank our way through every bar in Ocean City. I remember very little of the occasion except that both our paychecks were spent in three hours. I have a blurred visual fragment of talking to a girl at a bar booth surrounded by potted plants. She was deeply tanned and I kept trying to get her to show me her "white spots."

The drive home must have been horrifying but luckily neither of us could remember who was even at the wheel. Back in Rehoboth I went home and passed out, but Chuck still hadn't had enough. He drove to The Crystal Closet, a gay after hours club out on Route One. Don't ask me why he did this because Chuck was one of the straightest guys I ever knew. But desperate men will look for women anywhere.

There were only a few women in the bar, most of them bull dykes. Then he spied a lithe and stunning mulatto girl leaning against the back wall. He made a bee line for her. After feeding her two hours of passionate conversation and twenty dollars worth of drinks she told him she was a man. Chuck stomped out of the bar in disgust.

When he got outside his car wouldn't start. He kicked the tires in a rage and tied a red shirt to the door handle. It was five miles back to Rehoboth. Chuck got on Route One and started to hitchhike. A huge Cadillac pulled over and a plump foot kicked open the passenger side door. Chuck plopped onto the velvet upholstery with a sigh. Across from him sat a huge overripe mushroom of a human being. There must be bones under there somewhere thought Chuck.

"Rehoboth?" rumbled the blob. Chuck just nodded. Less than a mile down the road the fat man began to feel up Chuck's leg. He moved closer to the passenger side window but the hand stuck to him like velcro. They only had a few miles to go, hopefully the pudgy hand wouldn't make it to his crotch before the city limits. Just before the border of town, the fat man pulled off the highway and began tugging at Chuck's zipper. Chuck slapped his hand.

"Look," he said, "I'm not that kind of guy."

"Nonsense, all guys are."

"Why is it you homosexuals think all straights are really closet cases?"

"Look, I'm a judge, you got any parking tickets you need to get rid of? I can give you a clean driving record."

"No."

"Okay. Twenty bucks for a blow job."

"No."

"Okay. Fifty."

"If you give me ten, I won't go to the State News and report you."

It was an empty threat. They both knew that. But it killed the judge's mood. Both rode in silence. The judge dropped him off at our place.

Later that night when we were all asleep, the police raided our house and arrested us for disturbing the peace. We were dragged into the station and lectured all night about the evils of a bohemian lifestyle. At 9:30 in the morning they released us and we rushed to work and made frantic excuses about why we were late. The police wouldn't tell us who had filed the complaint but I'm pretty sure that if Chuck had shoved his dick in the guy's mouth he would have kept it shut.

Later that day when Chuck went to get his car from The Crystal Closet, the police had towed it. So he went down to the station again and paid sixty bucks to get it out of hock. As he drove it away Chuck noticed that his red t-shirt was still tied to the door handle.

One sunny day, me and some friends were at the beach walking along the surf, skirting the gaudy clotted crowds, when we saw a cluster of kids throwing sand balls at this one skinny blond haired boy who just stood there with his hands at his sides demurely taking it. When we tried to get them to stop they protested, "But he likes it! He asked us to."

We looked at the blond kid. He just smiled. So we picked up some sand balls and started throwing them at him too. After awhile our arms got tired and we walked on. By that time there was a line of passersby to take our place. The blond boy sat there beginning to bruise, loving the attention, his torso spattered with grime and mud. I wonder what he'll be like when he grows up.

Further down the beach some ten year old girls had built a twelve foot penis out of sand. They straddled the shaft and hopped up and down as if they were riding a horse. A fat woman was walking past a clump of washed up seaweed and Jim yelled, "Hey lady, you dropped your pussy!"

Chuck was at the Bottle and Cork that night getting his usual poor man's drunk. Since he was penniless, he would go to bars and look around the floors until he found enough change to buy drinks. Tonight he had found a ten dollar bill and was tying one on. By the time Sam caught up to him he was well into double vision and dancing like a yo-yo on quaaludes.

"You want to go with me to get some mushrooms? " asked Sam.

"Sure! What the fuck!" yelled Chuck.

They got in Chuck's car and Sam drove them to a sleeping residential area behind Ocean Mist condominiums. A-frame houses with aluminum siding, cracked sidewalks, bushy mulberry trees. They pull up to the dealer's house and go in. The living room is filthy, reeking of reefer and stale baby food. Emerging from the murk of the sofa is the dealer, a Sixties reject with a pubic hair beard and jittery amphetamine eyes that dart around the room. Chuck sits down in an easy chair and starts to pass out. Sam and the dealer haggle. It appears that Sam owes him some money from a previous occasion. Chuck is fading in and out. The haggling gets more heated. Chuck fades in. The dealer is shaking his finger in Sam's face. Chuck fades out. Chuck fades in. Sam is screaming at the dealer, gobs of spit flying into the pubic hair beard. Chuck fades out. Chuck fades in. Sam has picked up a chair and is swinging it around the room. He lets it fly and it sails through the living room window. Lights go on in the houses around the dealer's place. The neighbors, thinking someone is being murdered, call the cops. They show up and bust everyone. Chuck is still passed out. They read him his rights while he's unconscious. When he wakes up, he's in a jail cell.

They impounded Chuck's car. Sam, Chuck, and the dealer were all charged with disturbing the peace, vandalism, and assault. When the cops searched the house they found large quantities of marijuana, psilocybin mushrooms, and five unregistered weapons. So the three of them were charged with possession of narcotics with intent to distribute, and possession of deadly weapons as well. Plus when they examined Sam's record and found he was wanted in two states and living at Chuck's place, they charged Chuck with harboring a fugitive.

"I don't believe it," Chuck told me later. "Here I go to a bar, black out, and when I wake up I'm in jail with more charges on my ass than a Dillinger clone!"

Chuck got one phone call. He called his parents, explained his predicament, and they promptly disowned him. This left him with no money, no lawyer, no family, and no options.

The judge didn't know what to do with Chuck and Sam. He realized they were just scumbags who lacked the intelligence, sobriety, and organization to be real criminals. The dealer was the real catch out of this bunch. But what to do with these two? His cases were backed up. The prisons were overcrowded. What to do? In the end, Chuck had to spend two days in a Smyrna Prison cell with Sam. They were not perfect bedmates. For the entire forty-eight hours Sam bitched, "Chuck, how could you have gotten me into all this trouble?"

Finally on Wednesday morning they let them out and gave Chuck back his car. The two pooled their money and found they had fifteen dollars between them. They immediately spent all this on alcohol. For the next two days they went on a drunken binge, driving around northern Delaware and Pennsylvania, visiting relatives who stonefacedly put up with them for a meal but would then politely ask them to leave. On Friday night they ended up broke, starving, hung over and without gas in Wilmington, Delaware. A two hour drive away from the beach. So they went to a few shopping malls and stole hub caps. When they pawned these it made enough money to buy gas to get back to Rehoboth.

By the time Chuck had gotten out of jail and back to Rehoboth, he had lost his job at the T-Shirt Factory. He was also three weeks late for that month's rent and my roommates had had enough. They promptly kicked him out, hoping he'd take Sam's continual drunken presence with him.

Chuck moved his bags across town and stayed with a gay friend of his who lived behind the notorious Blue Moon. Chuck rented the couch in the living room. He had no money or job but promised he'd pay soon as he could. Three out of the four people who lived in the apartment were gay. The building was owned by a lesbian who lived two doors down. This was Rehoboth's pinkest section.

The Blue Moon is without question the most chic bar in Rehoboth. It's modern design is alive with sculptural nooks and crannies, and the pastel rooms shimmer with Maxfield Parrish hues of neon. Among its clientele are big name artists and senators. Exquisite gay men lounge around its porch in five hundred dollar outfits. These are the type of men who spend two thousand dollars in one weekend spree. Its regulars are the beautiful people of Rehoboth. Even the owner had a taste for the fine arts, and that summer there was an exhibit of Man Ray prints in the lobby. Chuck's apartment was about a hundred feet from the bar's back porch. When I went to visit him we would drink cheap six packs of Old Milwaukee while staring out the living room window at Washington men talking smooth and sweetly over a hundred dollars worth of mixed drinks.

The last person Chuck wanted to see was Sam, but there was no getting rid of him. Some sick parasitic magnetism made him stick to Chuck. Chuck made it quite explicit to Sam that his presence was not wanted there, but Sam would hear nothing of it, and marched right into his living room every night with a twelve pack of beer and began handing them out to Chuck's roommates. He never gave one to Chuck. And he'd sit there getting shit faced drunk insulting Chuck the whole time, telling everyone what a little limp dick Chuck had, how Chuck never could get it up, how he stole all Chuck's girls from him but it was really for Chuck's own good. Every night. The roommates didn't mind because Sam usually turned them on to beer and weed and besides, they liked to laugh at Chuck. Chuck had no choice but to sit there and take it.

But over the course of time things began to change. Sam stopped buying beer and began to mooch. Chuck had gotten a job in a jewelry store and now he usually ended up buying the beer that Sam slurped down in ever more excessive amounts. And Sam began to get violent. Occasionally, in a drunken fury, he'd smash something around the apartment. Chuck's roommates kept telling him to get rid of Sam. But what could he do? He explained to them that he didn't want Sam there in the first place, he hated Sam. His roommates would hear nothing of it. Sam was his friend and his responsibility. Chuck kept telling Sam he had to stop coming over, but every night he was there getting shit faced, passing out on the couch, making Chuck sleep on the floor, insulting Chuck every second he was there. Occasionally he'd drag women back from a bar and fuck them on the roommates' beds. One night Chuck threatened to call the cops on him and Sam belted him in the face with a beer bottle. Chuck hit the floor with a sound like a pumpkin makes when it's been dropped off a roof. Then Sam kicked him around for a while till he fainted. Finally he pissed on Chuck's unconscious face and bragged about it the rest of the night. Everyone in the room just looked at him squeamish. They were afraid.

The lesbian who owned the building had been complaining. Sam made a lot of noise late into the night. The roommates hated Sam so much they were beginning to hate Chuck too. It was definitely the time for violence. But Chuck just couldn't turn to that. His civilized upbringing and years in college had left him a hopeless pacifist. One night Sam took a crap and rubbed it all over Chuck when he was asleep. Things were reaching the breaking point.

Then one night Sam was already drunk when he came over. He walked straight in and helped himself to beer. He had been mooching for weeks. The night before, he had stolen fifty bucks from one of the roommates. We couldn't prove it but we knew who did it. Who else could it be? Before Chuck got there, Sam showed everyone a diamond engagement ring he had stolen from the jewelry store where Chuck worked.

"You should have seen that idiot," he said, "I was making him run around so much he didn't even see me take it. I could have cleaned out the whole place!"

Then he went on about what a horrible whiny wimp Chuck was, and how he couldn't get it up, and only went out with ugly girls. He was louder than usual. Every now and then he would lay his head back and holler at the top of his lungs. "Yeehaw! Yeehaw!" A violent redneck pustule screaming, "Notice me! Notice me!"

By the time Chuck arrived, Sam had switched his derision to homosexuals. This was not the right apartment for that topic. The three gay roommates sat there with a stony hatred hovering just beneath the viscosity of their faces. But Sam was too crude to notice.

"All them faggots," he said, "should be burned. Them queeny queers, nuke 'em! They ain't worth living. We should have kept the German concentration camps open for them. Hell, build new camps right here in this country. Fucking Fags! Fucking Fudgepackers! Fucking Dick Smokers!" he was screaming as loud as he could, "Kill 'em! Kill 'em all. We oughta burn down this whole goddamn queer neighborhood!

One of the gay roommates couldn't take anymore, and jumped up and socked Sam in the face. A vicious fight broke out. Everyone's face became camouflaged in blood. The landlady was banging on the front door screaming, "That's it! I've had enough of this noise and craziness every goddamn night! You all are evicted. I want you out tomorrow!"

"Shut up you fuckin' yeast breathed cunt licker," screamed Sam, "Fucking clam digger! Go back and lick yore Mama's twat you old dried up dyke!"

The landlady was shocked, she went to call the cops. Sam ran from the apartment with his shirt missing, streamers of blood all over his torso. He ran onto the back porch of the Blue Moon and began turning over tables, beating up faggots left and right.

"You faggots stole my money! You goddamn queers stole my money!" he kept screaming over and over. He broke two plate glass windows and had disappeared into the night by the time the cops arrived.

Chuck and his roommates were arrested for disturbing the peace. After they got out of the police station, they all went to the hospital for stitches. When Chuck went to work the next day, they fired him. It turns out a diamond engagement ring had been stolen during his shift the day before. They told Chuck he was lucky they didn't file charges against him.

When Chuck went home, his bags were sitting on the front doorstep. There was a note on them:

Chuck—
      You're out. Don't come back.
                          —The Roommates.

Two suitcases. All Chuck had left in the world, besides his car. Chuck brought the suitcases back to my place and asked if he could leave them there for a couple days. I said sure. Later that afternoon when nobody was home Sam came by and stole the suitcases.

Besides Chuck's clothes, the suitcases also contained his birth certificate, medical records, car title, car keys, high school diploma, all his legal documents, all his identifying papers. This meant that Chuck could no longer prove he was Chuck Hotchkins. On the other hand, Sam could prove that he was Chuck Hotchkins. And since Sam was wanted in three states, he did just that. Sam legally became Chuck Hotchkins. He took Chuck's clothes, his car, his birth certificate. After taking everything else from him, Sam had now stolen Chuck's very identity.

Chuck had no money, no job, no roof, no food. He didn't eat for two days. He couldn't find a job. He had never stolen anything in his life, but now it was a matter of survival. He went to the Seven-Eleven and bummed around the aisles for a half hour. Every day the management would take the stale bread, break it up into crumbs, and sell it in small paper bags as bird food. These bags were stored up front by the cash register. Chuck was poised against the back wall like a spring. He leapt and sprinted across the store, past the register, snatched a bag of bird food and ran out the front door. For sixteen blocks he ran as fast as he could. Then he hid in a hedge, panting, and stuffed the dull cardboard crumbs into his mouth. It tasted better than the Last Supper.

Chuck took Sam to court for the theft of his possessions. Amazingly, Sam showed up for the court date. The judge was a flabby mudslinging Baptist, an anchor for the withering old guard morality and a heap ah trouble for these new degenerates an perverts polluting this once pristine family haven. As soon as Chuck walked into the courtroom, he knew all was lost. The judge on the stand was the same one who had tried to blow him that night he was hitchhiking home from the Crystal Closet. Chuck stated his case. The judge didn't seem to be listening. He just sat on his bench playing with a rubix cube.

Sam went up to the judge and pulled him aside, "Look," he said, "I'm gonna confide in you. This whole case is a sham. That boy over there," he pointed to Chuck, "is a fairy who's been after my ass all summer. But me, I'm a straight heterosexual, girl lovin', red blooded American boy, and I wouldn't give him a piece. I mean can ya blame me, I mean look at him, would you even think of doing it with a greasy faggot like that?"

"No, of course not," said the Judge.

"I hear ya," said Sam, shaking his blond beard and hair up and down to prove his point. "But he can't deal with it, and has been in a jealous snit all summer trying to get back at me. Now your honor, do I look like the kind of guy who'd steal a penny from anyone? No, indeedy. I mean, this whole thing is so ridiculous, don't you agree?"

Yes, he did agree, and threw Chuck's case out of court. When Chuck tried to get the case retried, no one at the courthouse would listen to him. If Chuck wanted to do anything with the case, he had to hire a real lawyer. But Sam had taken all his money. On top of that Sam had taken Chuck's birth certificate and other papers to The Board Of Motor Vehicles and gotten a new license. Sam's photo next to Chuck Hotchkins' name. Sam was driving around town in Chuck's car, a car he now owned legally. The State now recognized Sam as Chuck Hotchkins. How could Chuck take himself to court?

Chuck somehow still had some friends left who lived out by the State Park and they said he could stay with them until he got his shit together. Chuck told no one where he was living, but somehow Sam found out, and would come out to the house and harass him. One night Sam drove by and shot out all their windows with a rifle. Another night when none of the men were there, Sam came by and tried to rape the woman who owned the place. He had smashed up the living room and had her cornered and beaten when Chuck got home. The two fell into a blood thirsty fight which smashed up the rest of the house.

They were swollen and bruised in the front yard. Sam's beard was red with blood. Since Sam had broken the phone, the woman had to run to a neighbor's to call the cops. The closest house was over a mile away. Chuck didn't know how long they had been fighting, but little pink dots were all over the edges of his vision. His nose was a spongy area that moved in any direction. But he didn't care, two of Sam's teeth were between his fingers. He had been waiting for this. It felt good. The blows went on, a staccato death dance in the salty night. Sand dunes surrounded them like a silent crowd as saw grass licked the blood from their legs. Chuck grabbed Sam's ear, it came out like a tuber pulled from gristle.

"Take that Vincent!" he yelled. But it just turned Sam into a blur, a whirling animal equation. Electric circles of pain were all over Chuck, their flashes brighter, brighter, brighter, till everything was black. Chuck was a pulpy puddle on the ground. Sam covered him with butane fluid, set him on fire, and drove away in Chuck's car. Luckily the police arrived less than a minute later and extinguished Chuck when the burns were only second degree.

The last time I saw Hard Luck Chuck, he was covered with stitches, bruises and burns. I was working at the Kite Shop when he walked, in displaying the hyperactive gestures and passionate eyes one only sees in certain mass murderers. I had never seen him so agitated. His last twenty dollars had been spent on a gun. For half an hour he explained with adrenaline phrases and grisly details how he was going to lure Sam out to a dark and deserted part of the beach with a pacifying offer of cocaine, and then murder him in cold blood. He would bury the body in Henlopen State Park. Way off in the dunes, a nameless grave, twenty feet deep beneath the cool sands. It wouldn't be that difficult. Sam was not the type of person anyone would miss. Little sparks shot from Chuck's eyes, and he was shaking his fist in the air as he left the shop. I knew that at their next meeting, only one of them would leave alive. But which one? I never saw either of them again.

Two years later, it was New Year's Eve. I was sitting

around with some friends, drinking to excess. The TV was tuned to coverage of Times Square. Drunken crowds swinging beer mugs in the air, streamers, confetti, and noise makers, that huge silver ball moving closer to midnight. The camera panned across the crowd. Lushes throwing up in gutters, smiling red faces, hazy eyes. Overflowing into the streets, everyone singing and screaming. Thousands of them. And there right in the middle of it, a little drunken speck, singing with the rest, was Hard Luck Chuck. I had no doubt. The camera lingered on his face for a good three seconds before it switched to a shot of the ball. Chuck Hotchkins, drunk off his ass but smiling like a motherfucker.

There's a feeling I get when I smell brine on the breeze and see the beaches plated dull silver beneath a summer moon. Occasionally you can hear the cries of whales out beyond the pulses of foam and you realize that somewhere out in that immense space of dark water, sharks glide through a blind world. The sand trembles between your toes and saw grass on the dunes whispers like a woman you knew so many drunken nights ago. People go off in different directions, like atoms lost in the abyss between stars, like autumn leaves long crumbled to dust, as all the memories of summer drift out upon the sea in search of storms.

BRICKS AND ANCHORS

Three months ago the crazy woman moved into our apartment. Since then we have been inundated by speed dealers, coke heads, LSD freaks, and a nonstop flood of punk mutants with hair of every color in Satan's Rainbow. Nose rings, needles, leather jackets, and comic books: the underground rolled over me like a bulldozer. Hungover, stressed out, with sleep a mere memory. Believe me, the bad die just as young as the good. They do too many drugs to last much longer. Within two weeks of her arrival we knew we wanted her out. But San Francisco law is slanted towards the renter. It protects them from many outside threats. Unfortunately, it doesn't protect them from other renters inside the apartment. We pushed hard to get her out and she fought back with a nonstop tempest of weirdness. Her name was Vicki Vicious and she was our Waterloo.

It seemed she knew everyone in the city who was involved in something illegal. Especially if it was drugs. In all my life, I've never looked for drugs as often as they were forced upon me during those three months. When you answered the door, you could always tell it was for her because their jaws were grinding and their teeth worn down. Either that or their pupils were as big as basketballs, about ready to roll out their heads and bounce off across the floor. These people were flying. And they were bringing me down because they had a tendency to walk out of the apartment with records, radios, and TVs. They showed up at all times of the day and night. There was no way to protect your belongings unless you sat in your room with a shotgun twenty-four hours a day. But after awhile, most of our valuables and expensive stuff was gone anyway.

She joined a noise band. Seven people and lots of amplifiers in the basement seven nights a week. Three girls banging on steel garbage cans in leopard skin clothes, playing instruments like a set of guitar pick-ups attached to a carburetor thrown into a grinding machine. So loud your feet shook on the upstairs floors. And an entire entourage of boyfriends, girlfriends, and groupies on drugs came with them. In stoned out trances they wandered through our rooms and picked up books, tapes, and whatever shiny trinket caught their eyes. But she couldn't keep the beat because she was always on speed when they jammed, so they booted her. Then there were just as many people over at the house, only they were all speed dealers.

The worst was when she invited Kidney to live with us. Kidney Stone was a clinical schizophrenic. Kidney performed demonic rituals. She was a good painter but could only work on canvasses when she was trance channeling with the Virgin Mary. So many voices and spirits flew through her head that she would often just sit in the hallway and moan in multiple personalities. Poltergeists had taunted her all her life. Kidney smeared shit on our walls and called it an act of art. For three generations her family had been plagued by the German Chocolate Goddess, a malicious female spirit that had brought down misfortune on her lineage even in the New World. Or at least that was what she said. I asked her if this meant Hershey's kisses were the kiss of death, and were chocolate Easter bunnies in on the conspiracy? Kidney read Aleister Crowley and claimed to understand it. She spent hours cross-referencing occult charts with astrological predictions. She claimed there were ectoplasmic flows in the hallway, puddles of Satanic goo on what appeared to be just clean hardwood floors. Demons attacked her at the dinner table and sent her screaming through the house. She could have the voice of a reptile or that of a frightened child. Once when we were eating my roommate offered her some bran muffins he had just cooked.

"Those aren't bran muffins, Jim," Kidney said. "They're little girls' breasts."

She tore off the ribbed paper that lined the bottom of one of the muffins and shook it between her fingers.

"And these," she said, "are their bras. And when you spread butter on them, that's the milk."

Another one of her famous monologues was about a quiet invasion of alien beings. These creatures looked vaguely human and walked around in rubber suits. Each one of them carried a wand or rod that they would touch to the back of unwary humans' heads. This would psychically drain away part of the victim's personality. Evidently there were so many victims of the Men With Rods in California that a support group had been organized and a twelve step program developed for them.

Now don't get me wrong. Stuff like this is entertaining when you see it in the movies or on the street. But when you have to deal with it on a day-to-day basis in your own house, it's a different story. Besides that, Kidney didn't pay rent and continually stole our food. Her demonic rituals complete with rings of candles, incense, and pyrotechnics often came close to burning the house down. We would have thrown her out on the street in a week were it not for Vicki's constant screaming threats. The two women had developed a strange symbiotic relationship. Kidney would come up with insane impractical ideas and Vicki would act them out. Like spray painting all the phones glow-in-the-dark purple. Like gluing pentagrams of sand to the walls, like shaving the cats. Whenever the other roommates flew into rages over these acts of weirdness and threatened to kick her out, she would be ooh so sweet to us and apologize profusely, and get us stoned, or give us a line of speed and set us up with her cute new wave girlfriends who talked about their butts all the time, and yes, they did have very cute butts and maybe Vicki wasn't so bad after all, a little weird to be sure, but maybe she was okay. And we'd walk back into the house and there'd be a dried-out dead squirrel nailed to the kitchen wall.

That dead squirrel turned out to be quite famous. It had belonged to a pale skinny man named Phlegm. He had found it run over on a roadside one day and was awed by its natural beauty. So he put it in a green plastic garbage bag, tied it shut, and carried it with him wherever he went. His favorite stunt was to take it into college dining halls and pass it around tables of ravenous eaters. They would fondle the bag and try and guess what was inside it. You can imagine their emotions when he told them what it really was. News of Phlegm and his mystery bag reached a bunch of musicians and they decided to call their new group The Dead Squirrel Dance Band. For awhile, them and Jerry's Kids were the biggest punk bands around. Unfortunately, one day Phlegm was run over by a Mack truck on the same road where he had found the carcass in the first place. Somehow, like Elvis's jawbone, the bunions of Jesus, or Dillinger's dick, Vicki had come into possession of the famous squirrel. True, it was an icon of history, but I still didn't want it on my kitchen wall.

Vicki was feces disguised as a human being, a parasite in girl's clothing. She did whatever she wanted and when anyone got in her way she screamed at them until they shrunk away. If the screaming didn't work, she threatened to kill them. If that still didn't move them out of her way, she would badger, insult, and degrade them until they hit her. Then she'd call the cops and have them take the obstacle away. Within two months of moving into any apartment, she had total control of the household and had transformed it into a pig sty, a fetid nest choked with her seedy belongings. Often all the other roommates would move out one by one, their safe haven polluted until it was unlivable. Vicki would replace them with her scumbag friends, unemployed people who partied all the time.

Things would be great for about two or three months. Then the utility companies would shut off the water, power, and heat because of delinquent bills. Or the landlord would stop by and freak out at the burn holes in the walls, shit stains on the kitchen table, or the shrunken head in the toilet, and Vicki would be tossed out on her ass. At most places she moved to though, the entrenched roommates just wouldn't put up with her shit, and she was kicked out in less than sixty days. In the two years she had been in San Francisco she had lived in seventeen different places. And she had never willingly left an apartment. Vicki might as well have glued a boot to her ass.

Then came the phone call. It came after she had lived there for six weeks and our house was descending into a musty pit of her tattered belongings and incense tainted clothes. Drug addicts were passed out on chairs in the front hall. Vicki got into screaming fights on the phone, received threatening letters. Sometimes people would knock on the front door in the middle of the night just to spit in her face when she answered it. In order to relieve the stress she had dyed her hair an extra three colors.

Jim answered the phone when it rang. "Now you don't know me," the voice said, "and it isn't necessary for you to

93

know my name. What I'm calling about is between Vicki and me. But I feel it's my duty to warn you about what's going on. A number of months ago Vicki was one of my roommates. She moved out on bad terms. Afterwards she repeatedly threatened me on the street and once hit me with a bottle. Then about two weeks ago she and Kidney broke into my house and stole thousands of dollars worth of my shit. I called the police of course, but since everyone was at work at the time of the robbery, there were no witnesses. There's only circumstantial evidence against Vicki. Now I've hired a private detective and your house is under surveillance as we speak. Look out your front window."

Jim looked out the front window.

"There's a Filipino guy in a '68 Firebird parked at the curb."

There was a Filipino guy in a '68 Firebird parked less than thirty feet from the house.

"Now if we can produce enough evidence," the voice continued, "the police might knock on your door some night with a search warrant. It might be a good idea to make sure there are no drugs in the house."

Jim looked over at a guy in a leather jacket passed out on downers in a pool of vomit next to the couch. Until Vicki was gone there would be no way to clean the house of drugs. She'd get busted for breaking and entering and we'd get carried along on charges of possession.

"I just wanted to tell you all so you won't be surprised if something goes down. This is just between me and Vicki. You all aren't involved."

"Thanks for warning us," Jim said.

The voice hung up. It didn't just involve Vicki. If the police got a search warrant we all would be implicated. Everyone in the house. This girl was going straight down the toilet bowl and she was taking us with her.

Our house is a moldering old Victorian, chock full of bad vibes piled up since the Sixties. It's at the corner of Haight and Ashbury, so it's had its fill of history. There's no telling how many people have overdosed in the basement. The walls are stained a dim gray by cigarette and marijuana smoke. The dry plaster is scuffed and smudged by bicycles, heels, and parties into a monochrome reminiscent of Franz Kline, an abstract vision of abuse. Red lights hang in the hallway. The street number has been done over in psychedelic paint. It appears to be wiggling when seen from a distance. Jam sessions and human lives flow through the building. Inside the doors, constant drug use sucks in all kinds of heavy energy. Rolling through this house there's a karma wheel sharp enough to cut off your fingers. Lots of crazy people have lived here. And there's chunks of their souls left over. We just try to be mellow and let the parade of strangers go on through. It's kind of like a wave you ride, one that curls around luck and personalities till it breaks and you move out. This place has seen the faces come and go and their imprints have been burned into the walls, like old photographs you hardly ever look at, memories that hang around and murmur until you only notice them as a minor feeling of unpleasantness. Artists and musicians have lived in these rooms and their songs still vibrate in the paneling. Occasionally during a jam session the old notes leap out of the walls and reinfect the new music, a rebirth in the pounding of the drum. The environment interacts with its creatures until it too becomes a living thing. Every young generation has its time and place. And this time belongs to us.

Kidney never cleaned anything. She rarely even bathed. Instead of washing her clothes, every month she dyed them a darker shade of black. She'd eat our food and leave the dirty dishes on the kitchen counter. After her rituals she often left the candles burning until they scorched holes into the floors. Cleaning up after her and Vicki was a full time job. One day I was mopping the kitchen while she sat at the table, cross-referencing the alignment of Saturn with the predictions of Nostradamus. When my mop picked up a chicken liver left over from one of her sacrifices, I blew a gasket.

"Kidney," I screamed, "why don't you ever do any fucking cleaning around this place?!?"

"What do you mean?" she replied, genuinely shocked. "Last week I cleaned up thirteen buckets of black tar from the kitchen and hallway. It was over a foot deep and all bubbling and throbbing. One of the biggest ectoplasmic flows I've ever seen. It took me most of the day to clean up all that sticky goo."

"Maybe," I said, "but couldn't you do some dishes too?"

A few weeks later when I was sweeping the hallway I found a Dixie cup taped to the wall. In the bottom of it was the dried residue of some foul smelling chemical.

"What's this thing doing taped to the wall?" I screamed.

"Oh, I put that there," Kidney said, poking her head out of her room. "There was a huge ethereal flow moving through that part of the house, so I took some turpentine, honey, and Coca Cola and put it in that cup. It's been transferring the negative energy away quite nicely. Don't worry, it'll only have to stay there another week and a half. By that time the full moon will come around again, and the place will be repurified."

Before I could say anything she ducked back into her room. I went back to sweeping. Whatever. Wasn't too much I could say. I'm all in favor of housecleaning.

Vicki and Kidney knew every witch in our neighborhood and believe me, the Haight Ashbury district is Witchcraft Central. They had an entire coven coming over twice a week, moaning and chanting in a pall of incense smoke thicker than a London fog. They began to cook up strange potions and brews in the kitchen pots. Nothing spoils your appetite worse than finding what looks like it might have been a bat wing congealed in the frying pan.

One night when I came home from work they wouldn't let me down the hallway to my room until I presented them my palms so they could determine whether or not I was a werewolf. I just pushed on past them yelling that I hoped I was a lupine ghoul so that at least they'd stay out of my apartment during the full moon. Spatters of candle wax covered the floors. Incense soot had stained the ceilings a charcoal black.

What was that voodoo doll doing in the refrigerator? But Vicki, I don't want to keep a human skull in the bathtub. I don't care if it's been spray painted such a pretty shade of green. No Kidney, it's not a good idea to have a campfire in the middle of the living room floor. I don't care if you put plastic down first, the entire house is made of wood and we'll all burn up. Yes Kidney, I'm sure there are people in this building who deserve to die, but I'm not one of them, and I think we'll let them die at their own pace, okay? Vicki, I'm not mad that you killed your pet tarantulas, I'm angry at you for putting them in the blender. I tried to be understanding, but every day it was something different.

The other two roommates, Jim and Steve, just hid in their rooms, and late at night when they were sure she was gone, they would come to me and beg me to get rid of Vicki. I was ready to give her the boot. But the first month we had tried giving her notice she screamed and threw things, smashed all her possessions, and set herself on fire. When she got back from the hospital with all those second degree burns and gauze patches, we felt sorry for her and let her stay another month. Our mistake. That was the month she moved Kidney in, and with her came the witches, the speed freaks, metal heads, and all Kidney's friends she had met at the institution. You know, the Medication Crowd. Wards of the State, people who still saw things no matter how much thorazine they had in them. Lovely bunch of people. Especially the ones who had shaved their heads to show off their lobotomy scars.

Kidney never lived in the house legally. She just showed up one day and kind of never left. Vicki told us she had a house guest coming to visit. One night I came home from work and the whole apartment was stinking of brimstone. I met Kidney at the front door dressed in full witch's regalia complete with pointed hat and broom, a dead lizard hanging from one of her hands. The first thing she did was hiss at me with a shrill reptilian cry. Vicki hung her head out of the door to her room and said, "Oh, hi John. This is my friend Kidney. She's going to be staying here for a week."

When the week became a month, and the house looked like a sorcerer's lair, we asked Vicki what was going on.

"Oh, I thought Kidney could just live here," she said.

"We never said that," me and Jim spit out incredulously.

"Well, you never said she couldn't live here," Vicki protested.

"You told us she was just visiting!"

"It's just that the people at her old apartment don't want her to come back."

"But we don't want her to stay here either," Jim said. "It's against our lease to have more than four people here."

"Well, who would ever find out?" Vicki stated.

"The landlord would," I replied, "and we'd all get kicked out. Plus, we don't want that many people living here. It's too crowded as it is."

"Why don't we take a vote on it?" Vicki suggested.

"We did, it's three to one, Kidney leaves," I said.

"But me and Kidney, that makes two," Vicki protested.

"It still doesn't make a majority," I said. "And besides, Kidney doesn't have a vote. She's not a roommate. She doesn't pay rent."

"Okay, okay," Vicki barked angrily. "I'll tell her she has to find a different place to live."

But Kidney kind of just stayed there for the next two months, the whole time carrying on with her group seances and full moon bacchanals. Her and Vicki constantly threw wild all night parties that kept me, Steve, and Jim up so late we were zombies on our jobs. When the neighbors are loud you can always call the cops on them, but it's hard to pick up that phone when you know you're bringing the pigs down on yourself. Of course, Kidney never paid us any rent.

There was a strain in Vicki's personality that was pure reptile. She even looked like a giant gecco dressed in leather clothing. Thin and wiry with a speed addict's body, when she smiled her upper gums glowed a neon red. Tattoos covered old needle tracks. Tribal markings surrounded an ankle, a dagger and rose on her breast, with the areola being the blossom. A skull leered just above her crotch, the pubes bristling from the lower jaw like Father Time's beard. She dressed black as a leather child gone bad, torn nylons, tight skirts, low necklines, a creature of the night. But what was most frightening was her eyes. The mascara hid something unstable, a fanged glimmer that hovered around her every mood. Like a snake that moves slowly in the heat you knew she could strike quickly and at any time. Her screaming fits leapt out of nowhere, could explode at you from a casual phrase. Snarling, clawing flights of degradation and below the belt insults that just made you want to crawl from the room to lick your wounds. Often we found ourselves apologizing for ridiculous hallucinatory offenses just to get her to shut up. If someone is that crazy and potentially violent, you just agree with them until you can get behind a locked door. Me and the other roommates got together late at night when we knew she was at a show or on an all night binge. In whispers we made plans for her expulsion. How would we get her out, and what if she came back and pulled off some horrible act of revenge?

I had come into some more disturbing information about Vicki. The source was one of her ex-friends. Evidently Vicki had gone out with Bud Luck, the lead singer of the Phlegmencos, for two years. It was a stormy up and down relationship with lots of broken glass. Both of them had bad tempers. One time they had an argument in the Phlegms' tour van while they were on the road. In the middle of the shouting, while the van was going sixty miles an hour, Vicki slid open the side door and tried to push Bud out onto the highway. If the bassist and drummer hadn't caught them, both would have been road pizzas. After another argument, Vicki took a hammer to Bud's head while he was asleep. She got in two good whacks and cracked his skull before Bud woke up screaming and threw her off him. According to rumors, Bud still had Vicki's '67 Thunderbird and a lot of her stuff. Whenever I asked Vicki about him the conversation rapidly deteriorated into a porridge of four letter words. Like all of her previous roommates, Bud was the biggest asshole she had ever known in her life. When I told my roommates these stories they were understandably upset. But how to get her out? Just give her notice, I said. Blame it on irreconcilable differences, the living situation just wasn't working out, clashing personalities and all that. Then be very nice to her for the rest of the month and pray she didn't break what was left of our valuables.

When we served Vicki notice she threatened to burn the house down. Kidney said she would cast the entire building into the deepest pit of Hell, and immediately began blurting incantations that would expedite the curse. Vicki threw pantyhose and crucifixes at us. She smashed her crystal ball and hit Jim in the head with a skull.

"I feel like I'm living with my parents," she screamed. "You can't tell me what to do. I'll do whatever the fuck I want, and nobody's going to stop me. Just because I'm a little strange, a little scary, nobody can handle it. They treat me like some kind of monster. Well, you all haven't begun to see how scary I can be! Those assholes talking about me all over town, they don't know shit! If you listen to them I'll fuck you up! I'll cut you! Cut your ear off so you'll be a real artist like Van Gogh! You all aren't artists, you're a bunch of fucking yuppies. You live your shallow, low lives. All you care about is money. So I can't pay the bills! Who cares? I'm cooler than anyone you'll ever meet." And she threw a handful of crystals at me.

"We're not trying to tell you how to live," I pleaded. "It's just that your lifestyle is causing the rest of us a lot of distress."

"My lifestyle is a fucking artform in itself," she screamed. "My life is so much more profound than yours. All you guys do is hide in your rooms and beat off all night. You all can't handle a real woman like me. I threaten you."

"Yes, you threaten us," I agreed.

Suddenly she became quite calm. Her face went tranquil and passive, from a hurricane to a still pond. "Yeah, I guess I have been kind of hard on you guys," she said sweetly. "I'm sorry. I'll be out at the end of the month. I guess it's just not working out. It's too bad. I really like you guys."

"We like you too," the three of us said simultaneously, our faces stiff with fear.

Vicki had grown up in Nebraska and the white trash upbringing never left her. All the leather in the world couldn't cover it up. Her mother had been a gold digger who used up three successively richer husbands. The last and apparently richest mate had owned a used car lot and white mansion complete with swimming pool. Unfortunately, after his demise, it turned out that his wealth had been a paper and plastic facade; he was in hock up to his dead ears. In her eighteenth year, Vicki and her mother were forced to move into a cheap rusty trailer. Vicki promptly cut out on her own, ready to use her mother's tricks. Her first catch was better than she could have imagined. A multimillionaire with all the trimmings. He owned six houses and two jets. Vicki was his hair dresser and confidante. She made about a hundred thousand a year in this role and quickly spent every penny of it. The millionaire set Vicki up with expensive hotel rooms and weekend trips to the Caribbean. She insisted that he was strictly gay, but I have a good feeling that some of the butt he was getting was hers. Two years down the road, the FBI put an end to this gravy deal. Turns out the millionaire was a key figure in the HUD scandal, and had embezzled thirty million dollars from the federal government. By the time he was in jail, Vicki had spent every penny she had to her name.

She spent her last thirty bucks on a bus ticket to New York City. There she worked as a nude dancer and made her way through a list of low life sugar daddies. The returns from these men got smaller and smaller. She dated singers in punk rock bands who were always borrowing money from her. Over the course of the next few years she journeyed through ever lower strata of society. She began stealing from strangers and friends in a desperate attempt to even the odds, but all this did was stack the deck against her. Now she was in San Francisco with a thirty day notice between her and the street. As far as I knew, she had no place to go. But we couldn't tolerate her any longer. Ex-roommates of hers kept approaching me on Haight street and telling me stories of how she had robbed things from them or set the beds on fire the last day she was at their houses. One night the guitarist for Sadistic Fart showed me a big scar on his cheek that he had gotten when Vicki hit him in the face with a chunk of petrified wood. All the stories of her outrageous thefts seemed to jibe with reality. Vicki owned thousands of dollars worth of leather clothing, boots, accessories, and top of the line fashion outfits. She had a lot of leather jackets that had to be worth at least three hundred dollars each. Besides that, she had six stereos, nine TVs, and enough expensive electronic equipment to start her own Radio Shack. Pretty good for someone who only worked part time at a head shop. Less than three weeks after she had moved in, I had already seen too many of her criminal friends and heard enough horror stories. I took what was left of my valuables and moved them into storage. But if what one of her previous roommates told me was true, not even this would help. After they had kicked Vicki out and changed their locks, she still broke in on Christmas day while they were away at their families' houses, and stole all their belongings. Dishes, albums, books, beds: she had gotten it all. When they came home from the holidays, their rooms were empty cubes. Vicki must have rented a moving van to get the job done.

Where did Kidney come from? From the wealthy suburbs of Chicago, evidently. Raised with a silver spoon in her mouth, and when her parents pulled it out, her sanity went with it. Her real name was Amy Jordan. Kidney Stone was the stage name she received after starring in an underground film where she was forced to eat an entire plate of giant slugs. When she was very young, her older brother was diagnosed as schizophrenic and committed to an asylum. Kidney and her parents went to visit him every weekend. Soon she became jealous of all the attention bestowed on her dysfunctional sibling. So she began to act crazy too. All of her creative energy went into calculated acts of madness. Of course her parents took her to a specialist. The therapist quickly saw through Kidney's sham and told the parents to ignore her. When they did, Kidney felt she had to act even crazier. But her parents still didn't seem to notice. This made her feel insecure and unworthy, so she continually threw herself into ever more desperate acts of absurdity. Like sewing all her teddy bears into a fur coat she insisted on wearing to church. Like dyeing the family dog hot pink. But if her parents ever noticed these stunts at all, it was only in the form of some brush off comment like, "That's nice, Amy, but have you done your homework yet?" thus sending her back to the lunatic's drawing board. This went on for years.

By the time she was in her twenties, Kidney realized that she didn't know how to act normal anymore. She had rehearsed so long that she had become the act. Her parents tried to send her to art school but it was hopeless. She could no longer fit into any kind of structured environment. After she dropped out she drifted through the cities, New York, Seattle, Philadelphia, her zany character and raw talent at painting often making her popular in underground circles. But her madness, whether it was an act or a reality, had become so advanced that it prevented her from getting anything together, even a stable living situation. Often, as soon as she began to settle into one place she would pick up on a whim and move to another state. These destinations were picked with the randomness of a roulette wheel.

For a while she lived with a demented filmmaker in Manhattan who forced her to eat small animals and grubs in front of the camera. This gave her a certain degree of underground fame, but her relationship with the director was terminated when he beat, raped, and stabbed her, leaving her for dead in a ditch near Syracuse. He had a cameraman record the entire act, and it went on to become one of his most famous scenes.

If she hadn't been crazy before, she certainly was now, from trauma if nothing else. She hitchhiked back to Chicago but her parents, bankrupt from her brother's treatments, could no longer deal with her and would not take her in. For a while she lived on the streets, doing lots of speed and LSD. Eventually the winds carried her to San Francisco. Many people had seen her eating gross things in the films so she quickly became popular, but her erratic behavior and a new fascination with witchcraft made her enemies just as quickly. Her complex but convoluted mind created a huge series of rituals and incantations that would give her revenge against those who had wronged her. But often halfway through the rites, the dopamine imbalance in her brain would cause her to forget what their original purpose had been. Most roommates she had couldn't deal with her, so her stay in any one apartment was usually very brief.

Then she met Vicki. Vicki thought Kidney was a genius, the best artist she had ever seen. She made a pledge to help Kidney in any way she could. The two became a team. Two nomads hell bent for eviction and mayhem. Vicki made Kidney do horrible things. Sometimes when they were really down and out, Vicki even convinced Kidney to sell her body so they could buy food. Kidney knew Vicki was evil, but she didn't care. Everyone Kidney had ever known had kicked her out, ignored, raped, or beaten her. In many ways Vicki was the first real friend she had ever had.

Two weeks before the end of the month, Vicki announced that she and Kidney were not going to move out. I

103

told her calmly but firmly that she didn't have any choice. She had been given her thirty days notice and she was going to have to stick to it. Kidney had no say in the matter. She was an uninvited house guest and therefore had no renter's rights. Vicki screamed that we were a bunch of unfair yuppie bastards. I said that might be true, but she was still moving out. She let out a shrill inhuman squeal and ran into the bathroom. From the toilet she grabbed an unflushed turd and began rubbing it all over the wall. When Jim tried to stop her, she smushed the shit into his face. He lifted his fist to put her lights out, but I grabbed his arm and demanded that he leave the house. Don't ask my why, but he obeyed me. Maybe something told him that she wasn't worth a homicide charge. When Jim left I tried to reason with her. She began to throw chairs. Into the wall, at me, a stool went through the kitchen window.

"You fucking yuppie bastards," she screamed. "You all don't know how to handle a real artist like me."

"What's artistic about rubbing shit on the walls?"

"There's more profundity in that one act than you've had in your entire life. You just can't see the beauty of shit."

"No, I can't! It's fucking inhuman! Animals don't smear shit on the walls of their dens. You're lower than a goddamn animal."

"Well, you all are yuppie pigs, you all should wallow in shit."

"Wallow in your own shit in your own house. But get the hell out of ours," I screamed.

"This is my house," Vicki sneered, "and I'll do whatever I want here."

"No, you won't," I said. "This house belongs to all of us, not just you. You can do what you want as long as it doesn't interfere with us. And you stepped over that line when you started slinging shit. All you can see is your own fat slug self and your own selfish needs."

"That's because I'm more important than you all," she howled. "I'm cooler than all of you all put together. All you all do is hide in your rooms..."

"Maybe we're hiding from you."

"You all are just hiding from me because you can't take

104

how hip and beautiful I am. You all just sit in your little holes jerking off thinking about me, burying yourselves in piles of spermy kleenex. If it weren't for your right hands you all wouldn't have any lives. You all think you're fucking artists, you aren't artists, you're fucking yuppie jerk offs who are so jealous of me you can't stand it!"

"What we're talking about has nothing to do with art, Vicki. It has to do with living together in a common house. It has to do with consideration for others' feelings, concepts which are obviously incomprehensible to you. And besides, what art do you do anyway? You don't paint, draw, or write. And the only band you were in, which was a noise band, you got kicked out of. What art do you do?"

A chair went flying over my head. "Destruction is my art," she screamed. "Breaking things is my creation. I'll destroy everything you own. As soon as you walk out that front door, I'll set it all on fire. When you come home there'll be just little pieces left."

"The fuck if you will. I'll have you arrested."

"Oh, will you? Then why don't you go ahead and do it. Go on, John, Mr. Tough Guy, call the cops. See if I care. Go ahead, call them, dial 911."

"I just might."

She overturned two lamps and smashed three ashtrays, then she opened a kitchen cabinet and began throwing dishes onto the floor. I grabbed her hand to stop her and she looked at me with a glare of pure lust and hatred.

"Go ahead, hit me," she whispered. "I know you want to do it. You want to do it so bad you're probably getting a hardon."

I cocked my fist back and tightened the muscles up. I've never wanted to hurt someone so bad. But no. That would be sinking to her level. In a sick way I would be giving her just what she wanted. I let my hand drop to my side.

It was obvious that she was very disappointed. "You faggot," she hissed. "You're no kind of a real man. You fucking wimp. A real man would have hit me."

"And you would have called the cops," I said.

"Smart boy."

She continued smashing dishes. She smashed the

bowls and glasses with such a fury that she hopped up off the floor with each throw. The whole time she was screaming at the top of her lungs, a mindless angry beast.

"You don't know anything about me," she shrieked, "you don't know who I hate or want to hurt. I think about hurting people every day, every minute. There are lots of people I'd like to kill!"

When she said that I calmly walked out the front door and called the police from the pay phone across the street. When the officer showed up, I let him into the apartment.

Vicki sat silently at the kitchen table. She was calm, almost trance-like. She answered all the officer's questions in a passive, emotionless monotone.

"Why are you all here?" she asked. "Nothing has happened."

The shattered pieces of debris all around her told a different story.

"Your roommate here says you smeared excrement on the walls," the officer said. Her face lit up to a spark, a flush of the previous rage returned.

"Oh, did he say that? Excrement? Well, that's very fucking eloquent, John. You're a real poet."

"Well, did you rub excrement on the wall?" the officer asked again.

"It wasn't excrement, it was feces. That's shit, Shit, SHIT!"

The officer rolled his eyes. Just another night in the Haight Ashbury. Vicki lapsed back into her trance-like state. The officer asked me to step out front for a moment. We left Vicki in the kitchen, murmuring to herself. When we were out on the street, I asked him if there was any way to get her out of the apartment.

"Well, we can't move her out by force," he said. "There's a lot of stuff broken in there, but besides the two of you, there were no witnesses. If she had burned something it would have been different. But, at this point, we don't have enough evidence to establish an immediate threat to the property. If you could do that, she'd be out in forty-eight hours. Is she leaving at the end of the month?"

"She's supposed to," I said glumly.

"Well, my advice to you is to try and be very nice to her for the next few days and maybe she'll move out when she's supposed to."

"And if she doesn't?"

"She could pull a rent strike. In that case it would take three to six months to have her evicted."

"By which time the rest of us will have moved out to preserve our sanity," I moaned. "I guess I'll have to be real nice to her."

"I don't know," the officer said as he climbed back into his squad car. "I'd be careful with her. I don't think she's playing with a full deck."

Like tell me something I don't know, I thought, as he drove away.

That last week was pure hell. Vicki's threats and screaming fits were incessant, a non-ending stream of abuse and below the belt degradations. And the whole time I just had to bear it all smiling. I exuded pleasantness and continually complemented her on the beauty and sophistication of her artistic pursuits. Of course I never left the house the whole time. To do so would have been like filling the place with gasoline and striking a match on my way out the door.

Me, Steve, and Jim bought locks for our bedroom doors. Vicki would scream and deride us when we were locking them. Didn't we trust her? Did we think she was a thief? Why were we taking the word of strangers over her own? We were the real criminals in this. How dare we listen to gossip. We just said nothing and turned the keys in the locks.

Right before the end of the month Vicki lost her job. When I asked her why it had happened, she said that her boss at the head shop was an asshole. She had no money and lived on a diet of ramen noodles and soup kitchens. She had also hurt her leg. She claimed it happened while slam dancing at a Pus Cocktail show. A friend of mine told me what had really happened. An old enemy of hers had seen her on the street and kicked her leg until she could hardly walk, but by this time I had no idea who was telling the truth. I just wanted her out of the house. Now she hobbled about the dim rooms stacked near to the ceiling with her tattered belongings, screaming at the walls and beating the mangy cats with her cane. Kidney just hid in her room and prayed to Satan.

Why did we let Vicki move here in the first place? It's the same old story. Two days before the end of the month and we were still short one roommate and their portion of the rent. A time of household desperation. Vicki had gotten our address from a roommate referral service. The first time we met her she was wearing a normal t-shirt and jeans. She was sober, well groomed, and articulate. What she liked best about the place was that it seemed like a quiet apartment where she could get a lot of reading done. Rent was due in less than forty-eight hours. She seemed as wholesome and prim as a Fortune 500 secretary. Things like this happen quite often in the renters' world. You meet someone, and in ten or fifteen minutes you have to make a character assessment that will affect your personal environment for months to come. She had the money and was ready to move in. We gave her the key. Our only fear was that we would be too wild for her. So it was quite a surprise when the Republican secretary left and what returned to move in the next day was a crazed leather freak covered with tattoos. When she had applied for the room, her hair was jet black, but the next day it had been redyed to its official military green hue.

The week that Vicki and Kidney were supposed to move out I was left on my own. Jim was on vacation to New Orleans for Mardi Gras, Steve just disappeared. Living with Vicki was pushing him closer and closer towards alcoholism, and he was wont to disappear for two day periods without any warning. When he returned, he was always bleary eyed and frazzled. Two days before Vicki was to vacate, he walked out the front door with a bottle of tequila and we didn't see him again till it was all over.

But I wasn't ready to just give up on the place. True, the apartment had degenerated into a pigsty where all our valuables had been smashed, but it was my pigsty. It had become a territorial thing, Vicki and I were like two lions on the veldt, fighting it out for the shade of the only tree. And I wasn't about to give up to that bitch. She had invaded my living space with all the subtlety of a strep virus and turned it into her own private cesspool. I had been pushed into my room and almost out the rear window but I wasn't going any further.

Time to make a stand. I put extra padlocks on all the bedroom doors. I invited my friend Chaos to stay at the house while Vicki moved out. He would act as a strong arm man and a buffer to protect our possessions. And he worked cheap. All he demanded was a bed and a steady supply of rum and marijuana.

When she saw the padlocks go up, Vicki began to scream curses at me.

"Don't you trust me?" she asked.

"No."

"How come?"

"Two nights ago you said you would destroy all our belongings and fuck us up."

"But I didn't mean that."

"It was what you said, and you were throwing chairs at me to emphasize your point."

"But I wouldn't hurt your stuff," she said with a sinister smile.

"Too late, you already have. You broke most of the dishes in the kitchen."

"But I'm not a violent person," she pleaded.

"Quote. You don't know who I'd like to kill. There are lots of people I'd like to hurt. Unquote."

"You heard that from someone around town. You've been listening to gossip again. How can you believe that trash?"

"You said that yourself, two nights ago."

"I did not."

"Yes, you did. Quote. Destruction is my art. Unquote."

"Oh."

It was too late for apologies and they would have been ridiculous coming from her. She had just as much hatred and violence left in her. We both knew it. She was still cooking up fantastic plans of revenge. It was no secret. We both walked back to our rooms and began making separate plots.

For a couple of days an uneasy quiet reigned over the apartment, but events reached a fever pitch the night before Vicki moved out. Around midnight there was a knock on the front door. Vicki and Kidney were out on another all night LSD binge trying to fuck the lead guitarists of no-name punk rock bands. The guy at the door was young but haggard, with the look in his eyes of one who has been screwed over one too many times.

"I've come to warn you about Vicki," he said.

"Believe me," I replied, "I don't need to be warned. I already know. But I'm always anxious to hear more information. Come on in."

He walked in and looked around the hallway at the smashed furniture, the tattered feather boas, psychedelic sands that glowed in the shape of pentagrams glued onto the floor, pieces of skulls, voodoo dolls, and crystal balls lying everywhere.

"Yeah," he said, "our place looked like this just before we kicked them out too."

"You lived with both of them? How horrible. I thought you might have gotten away with living with just one."

"They come as a pair. It's a weird symbiotic relationship. Vicki always moves in first. Then she moves in Kidney once she's established a base camp. Every place Vicki has lived in this town has ended up with both of them. Kidney's the bigger parasite. Once she gets in your door, it's almost impossible to get rid of her."

"Like fleas or roaches," I said.

"Yeah. It takes at least a month just to explain to her what the word EVICTION means. Even once people manage to kick out Vicki, it still takes at least another two or three months to get rid of Kidney. But by that time Vicki has found her a new place to stay."

"Sounds like the voice of experience," I said.

"It is. They lived with me and I'm three thousand dollars poorer as a result of it. Which is why I came by to warn you. Whenever they leave a place they tend to walk out with everything that's not bolted down."

"I was afraid of that. That's why I've put locks on all the doors and have a friend watching the place."

"Good idea, but it might not be enough. They have a tendency to come back and rob their previous houses. I'm talking Breaking and Entering. Vicki is the prime suspect in two burglary cases around town. There's a handful of warrants out for her arrest in New York City. These are dangerous

110

people."

"How can she keep doing this?" I said. "Going around town robbing people and not getting caught?"

"It can't go much further," he said. "She's got a fat line of enemies all the way across this town and nowhere left to go. She's used up all her friends. Once she leaves here she's either going to a flophouse or back to her mother's in Nebraska."

"She just keeps going down..."

"But she never hits the bottom," he said, "which is unfortunate, because she drags a lot of people down with her. Myself included. I even hired a private detective to try and help me get some of my stuff back."

"So it was you who hired the Filipino in the Firebird."

"Yeah. But he could have been employed by any one of about fifty people."

"I know that," I said. "Is the house still under surveillance?"

"No," he replied. "I want to try and get my stuff back under my own terms."

"Well, I just want her out of my house," I said.

"Understandable," he said. "But there are a lot of people around town who have their stolen belongings in this apartment here now, and they'd like to get them back. My friend Sandra lost three leather jackets to Vicki worth about two hundred bucks each."

I knew he was telling the truth. I'd been in Vicki's room. In a wax spattered pile in front of her closet were about thirty or forty leather jackets, most of them new, roughly three or four grand's worth of dead animal hide all put together. A lot more than anyone unemployed could afford to buy.

"Look," I said, "she's supposed to move out tomorrow. I just want that to go off without a hitch. But I have no love for these girls and I think you're telling the truth. If you can come up with some way to get back some of your stuff you're welcome to try, but I want no part of it."

"We were thinking of getting Vicki forcibly committed to a mental institution for seventy-two hours."

"No. I want her out of here in less than twenty-four. Anyway, wouldn't it be easier to commit Kidney?"

"She's too passive. Vicki's the violent one. Cops will only lock up a screamer, not a zombie. Besides, you can't predict how Kidney will react. That makes it hard to manipulate her. I should know, I went out with her for two years."

"You went out with Kidney?!?"

"Yeah. But she wasn't this schizophrenic back then. She comes and goes. It all depends on the chemicals in her brain. I tried to take care of her. She's a good painter and I got her a couple shows, worked as her manager, sold a few canvases for her. I also got her on SSI. That's how she stays alive, gets six hundred a month from the state. And that's another thing I wanted to warn you about. I think Vicki's been stealing Kidney's welfare checks from her."

My God, I thought, the parasites feed upon the parasites. "I'm worried about Kidney," he continued. "I want to make sure Vicki doesn't steal even more of her stuff when she moves out tomorrow."

"How would you get Vicki committed?" I asked.

"Easy," he said. "Every time she sees me she gets violent. Starts throwing things. Tries to claw my eyes out. All we gotta do is call a cop and have him standing by to witness it when I knock on your front door and she answers it. Soon as something hits me in the head they take her away, and me and my friends go through her stuff while she's in the brig."

"Bad idea," I said. "Then she gets out, comes home, finds a lot of her stuff missing, and I get blamed for it. Real bad idea. No. If you want, you can help me move them out tomorrow, but you aren't pushing anyone over the deep end in my house. If she attacks you that's her business, but whether she's here or not, Vicki's stuff is going out the front door before midnight tomorrow."

"And what about Kidney?"

"She's going too. If I have to throw her stuff out piece by piece, she's still leaving. I can't take it anymore."

"I might be able to put Kidney up at my place," he said.

"That's fine. Because she can't stay here."

"Okay. I'll be back tomorrow."

"I don't even know your name," I said.

"Billy. Billy Zygote. See you tomorrow." And he slipped off into the night.

Who was this stranger who had come in the middle of the night to warn me about mad women in my house? Strangers had begun to come out of the woodwork to relate tales of terror about Vicki and Kidney. These women had painted a path of destruction across town, indeed, across the entire country. Everywhere they had been they took more than they gave, psychic leeches bloated with bad luck, spilling it on everyone they touched. I was in a serious situation, one I hoped to get out of without sustaining physical injury. I had already given up on my possessions. People had begun to leave cryptic messages on our answering machine, warnings about Kidney and her practices in demonology, tales of stitches and hospitalizations due to Vicki and her affection for throwable objects. So many messages had piled up on the tape that Vicki no longer tried to erase them. On one level I think she even took a secret delight in having us hear those messages. She was scary and she knew it. It was her strength. Her island of threat in the middle of the foundering chaos that was flushing her life. Like a clawing mindless beast, she got her way through the pure strength of her frenzy. Billy had told me stories: the time Kidney broke a bottle on his face because he caught her squatting down and urinating on a human skull, the time Vicki injected her cats so full of speed that they ran around as thrashing blurs until their little kitty hearts exploded.

So many people had told me so much conflicting information about these girls that I had no idea who was telling the truth anymore. Were Vicki and Kidney raging psychos, Public Enemies #1 and 2? Or were they just misunderstood victims of vicious rumors? I couldn't tell anymore. Maybe everyone was lying. I needed answers, and I knew where to get them. From Vicki's ex-boss. Ruth, the manager of Bong World, was an old friend of mine. When I was in Third Leg, she had gone out with our drummer. Now I needed to pump her for some serious information. If nothing else, she could tell me the real reason Vicki had been fired.

When I buzzed her apartment, Ruth made me walk out into the middle of the street so she could see me from her second story window before she would let me in. When I got up to her flat, it was obvious that she was flustered and nervous. Her hands were shaking, and all the ashtrays in the room were overflowing with cigarette butts.

"I'm sorry," she said, "it's just that I've been under so much stress lately."

"Me too," I said. "Look Ruth, I need some information about someone."

"Who?"

"Vicki Vicious."

A pained look blemished her face.

"What do you want to know about her?"

"Anything. Anything at all," I said. "It's very important."

"Well, she's why I'm all stressed out. You see, I had to fire her a couple weeks ago."

"I know."

"How did you know?"

"She's one of my roommates."

"You poor soul. Then you must be in big trouble."

"That's what I'm trying to find out. Why'd you have to fire her?"

"Well... over the course of the past month Vicki got more and more... unstable on the job. She got really bitchy and sharp with customers. And then right before the end, she couldn't control herself at all. She would yell and scream at people in the store, in a really violent and degrading manner. Kept going off on these horrible tantrums about their sex lives. Now I've known Vicki for a couple years, and she was never an angel, but lately she's been getting worse. Much worse. I've never seen her this violent. It's scary."

"Sure is. What finally broke the camel's back?"

"One day she just blew up at some guy out of the blue. I mean he was really polite and well dressed, totally uptown. And she just started screaming and yelling at him, calling him a "fucking yuppie." That's the way it is with her, it's always the fucking yuppies' fault. Then she picked up a hundred dollar glass bong and threw it at him. Just missed him and shattered all over the wall, and he goes running out into the street, scared shitless calling for a cop. That left me no choice. I had to fire her right then and there. The head shop gets

114

enough flack without that kind of shit going down. So I took her out onto the sidewalk because I was afraid when I told her she'd start smashing up stuff in the store. It was a good idea because she had a complete freakout. Threatened to kill me and burn down the store and my house. She even threatened to come rob my house after she had burned it down. Then she went for my throat, started strangling me, tried to smash my head through the front window. She was banging my face into the plate glass, and I would have gone through too, if the cops hadn't shown up. As soon as the lights and sirens pulled onto our street she took off running. I haven't seen her since. But I've heard from her. Every couple of nights she calls me up with a death threat. I'm really worried. I can't sleep, I'm stressed out, losing weight. Every time I go to the store I'm completely terrified and paranoid, worrying that she'll come in there and start smashing things up, or worse, show up with a gun. Someone smashed the front window two nights after I fired her, but I can't be sure it was her."

"Probably was. I'm trying to get her out of my house. You got any advice for me?"

"Move out first. That woman is completely out of control, she's dangerous. If you want to, you could stay here for awhile. "

"Sorry. Thanks, but I don't give up that easy. Plus it would give her too a good target to have two of her worst enemies under one roof."

"Suit yourself. But if I was you, I'd move to Kalamazoo. I won't feel safe till that girl's behind bars, which hopefully won't be much longer."

"Oh, by the way," I added, "you know some dude name ah Billy Zygote?"

"Yeah. He's just as crazy as she is."

"Great. They're all crazy I guess."

"Pretty much."

"Thanks for the info," I said and got up to leave.

"Good luck," she replied in a worried quaver.

I walked home sunk in a total depression bigger and colder than the fog obscuring the city. My bravado in front of Ruth had been completely false. Well, I had wanted answers, and I got them. Got them in spades. Nothing like finding out your worst nightmare really is your worst nightmare. When I got home and saw that Vicki had nailed one of her cats' heads above the knocker on the front door, I realized it was time to give up all hope, because I was about to re-enter the tyranny of the dream.

I had chosen Chaos as a strong arm man for more than just his physical power. He was a cool one. With an almost eastern Zen calm he knew how to use force only where force was necessary. I'd never seen him lose it. Even in the middle of a brawl at a bikers' party once, I had seen him stern faced and calculating in the thrashing bodies, fending off blows, and only punching enough people to clear a way out of the violence. He never started fights but he was good at finishing them. Also he seemed to have some kind of invisible antennae. Chaos could tell when something dangerous was about to happen. His ears would prick up, and he'd go quiet and look around intently, every nerve steely and on edge, waiting. And sure enough, a car would crash into a telephone pole, some drunk would come out of an alley swinging a bat, or a gang of hubba heads would drive by shooting. It was really uncanny. He always said he could feel it like a change in the vibration of the air. I don't know how he did it, but he was good to have around.

Chaos wasn't the biggest of dudes, but he was in tip top shape, with just enough karate and LSD under his belt to be a formidable foe. His brawls were won not through brute force, but with a thrashing almost animal frenzy. He was a crazy motherfucker and anyone who messed with him found that out quick. But he wasn't a violent person. In fact he was quite calm and mellow, preferring meditation and camping to contact sports and raising hell.

"The important thing is to have power, but not necessarily to use it. Employ it only when you have to, otherwise you'll lose it," he once told me. Another thing that made Chaos a valuable choice was that he had lived in poor bohemian households in San Francisco for over ten years. He knew how to deal with crazies. During those last few days with Vicki and Kidney he was all that held me together. He kept talking me down from incredible heights of stress, mellowing me out with smooth words and logic. Over and over he drove into me the importance of not breaking.

"Remember," he said, "that under all the black magic and leather, Vicki is still just a piece of white trash from Nebraska. And Kidney is just a lunatic."

"I know, I know," I would stammer. "I'm not worried about the hordes of Satan. What scares me is two small women who might stab me in the back with a big butcher's knife."

"That's why you got me here to watch your back," he said.

"And I'm damn thankful for it," I replied.

"Good, why don't you roll me another joint then?"

As I was rolling it, I said, "Man, Chaos, I'm sorry I got you mixed up with these crazy people. They're driving me out of my mind. But you don't have to stay here if you don't want to. I mean, you don't have any real stake in this."

"Look," Chaos said, "I've known you and Jim for years. You're my friends. Whether you're right or wrong, even if you're wrong, I'm going to stick by you all and do what I can. You're the people in my life and there aren't any others. We're a group and we gotta watch out for each other and protect ourselves from other groups. You shouldn't even question why I'm here. I don't really have any choice in the matter."

I smiled, lit up the joint, passed it to him, and felt calm for the first time that day.

Some nights later, around three a.m., Kidney was walking up and down the hallway in the darkness, hissing like a giant reptile. Occasionally she would call out to Satan in a voice of pure nihilism. When he did not answer she made up her own answers, talking to herself in a male personality with a voice harsh and bearded, except when it was punctuated with shrill demonic laughter. These one person plays would go on for a few minutes, but slowly the Prince of Darkness would drift out of her and she would stand frozen as a wax statue, in a catatonic state for about a quarter of an hour. Then a female spirit would visit her.

The goddess would conduct an interrogation of Kidney and she lied to it continually. Especially when the goddess asked about Satan. That's when I knew Kidney was truly insane. Kidney would be possessed by successively lower status poltergeists until she thought she was a reincarnated weasel and would sit on all fours in a corner, snarling at Vicki's cats who fanned around her in a half circle meowing. In a Buddhist nightmare she would work her way down to the ghost of a worm, as she flopped around on her stomach, in front of the horrified eyes of the cats, pretending she had no arms or legs while sucking at pieces of dirt on the floor.

The day that Vicki was supposed to move out she wore a sinister Lizzie Borden grin, a threatening piece of meat that exposed her sharp teeth. Her and Kidney owed us five hundred dollars in unpaid bills, and through all of my negotiations for payment I felt as if I was dealing with a taut mousetrap. She said she would pay them later that day and I foolishly agreed, not realizing that this would give her time to move out most of her possessions.

An anorexic vampire showed up to help the girls move out. All his front teeth were chipped into a snaggle toothed leer that was little more than an extension of his colorless face. So few muscles existed on his body that the bones stretched his skin almost to the breaking point. Plus he had a nervous speed freak twitch that made his crossed eyes goggle in odd directions. With all the civility of a drooling corpse he shook my hand with fingers cold and limp as dead octopus tentacles. In a sick way he reminded me of Count Chocula or the demon in *Nosferatu.*

He had an enormous '65 Cadillac with curtains in the rear window. The trunk alone was big enough to hold a coffin. We began filling it with the huge piles of Vicki's possessions. She wasn't around to help but I didn't care. Anything it took to get her out. As I threw a Kon-Tiki death god idol into the back seat, the vampire yelled, "Hey, watch it, I don't want to rip up my nice upholstery. That's real suede."

I looked at the seats. The fabric was so sun bleached and dry rotted that you could no longer distinguish the original pattern. Gaping tears in the seats bulged outward with yellow foam. Whatever. I loaded the rest quite gently. By the time we were done the trunk had to be tied shut. African masks, fishnet stockings, and broken TV sets hung out of all the windows. When the vampire got into the driver's seat he looked like an astronaut boxed into his space capsule, stuff was piled up to the ceiling all around him. He left and came back and we filled up another carload. And another. And another. All in all we filled up five carloads worth of Vicki's belongings. And it still took another two pickup truck loads to finish moving her out. This from a woman who lived in one ten by ten foot room.

As the day went on I found I could walk through the hallway again, and could use the toilet without having to take some of Vicki's possessions off the lid first. Load by load our apartment was becoming ours again. But what was left was an empty white cube. During her stay, Vicki had slowly but surely thrown all our furniture and paintings away, and replaced them with her own thick layer of junk. It had been done by steady subtle degrees, in such a quiet fashion that we had not even noticed being moved out of our own house. Towards evening, when most of Vicki and Kidney's stuff had been moved out, I saw that no remnant or icon of the other three roommates remained anywhere in the common space of the apartment. Not a chair or magazine or even a drawing on the wall. The only possessions that me, Jim, or Steve had in the house were securely locked behind the padlocks on our bedroom doors. If we had given Vicki another month, she probably would have had those rooms too.

It only took two pickup truck loads and three carloads to move Kidney out, and I think that up until the end she didn't even understand what the term "move out" meant. I just went up to her that morning and said, "You are moving out, TODAY. No excuses. No ifs, ands, or buts. Out. Today."

"But you can't just move someone out of your house," she whined.

"You can if they just moved themselves in without permission," I replied.

"But it's such short notice."

"Look, Kidney," I shook my finger at her, "we've been telling you to get out for a month and a half. You were never supposed to live here in the first place. It's against our lease to have this many people living here. We've given you five one-week notices and ample time to vacate. We've been as pleasant and understanding as any human beings could be, but you've pushed us to the limit and taken total advantage of us the whole way. Any normal person with half a spine would have pitched you out on the street weeks ago. And that's where you're going now. If you have some place to go that's fine, but your stuff is going out the door no matter what. This is it, Kidney. No questions. No answers. Later!"

She shuffled back to the guest room and began to pack up her stuff. For the rest of the day I had to exert a continual personal force on her, like a battle of egos, a constant karmic push that subliminally moved her outward. She was moving out, but getting her to pay the bills was a different story.

"Just because I didn't pay rent doesn't mean I should have to pay bills," she declared, as if there were some moral logic behind the statement. I just rolled my eyes. Oh, if only my other roommates were here to help me deal with these women.

That evening as the sun began to set, Vicki exploded into a shrieking banshee, degrading me, Chaos, and the entire human race. Most of her stuff had been moved out, so now she didn't feel a need to hide the fact that she had no intention of paying off the big stack of bills she owed us. She lorded it over me like a matter of pride. But even though she wasn't going to pay her gas, electric, and phone costs, she demanded her damage deposit paid back in full. I said no way. Her and Kidney had trashed the place. They had used up their deposit and then some. Spray paint on the walls, burn holes in the floors, gooey piles of black magic leftovers lying everywhere. They weren't getting jack shit back till they paid what they owed us. Besides, the new incoming roommate hadn't paid me his damage deposit yet. There was no money to give her.

"You're trying to rob me," she screamed. "You're a liar and a thief. This place was a shit hole till I moved in and fixed it up."

"Yeah, you converted it from a shit hole to a cat box. Now there are kitty turds on all the floors and trash everywhere."

"Ha! You don't know how lucky you are to have lived with a great artist like Kidney. She's gonna be greater than

Van Gogh."

"Does that mean I can cut off both her ears!?" I screamed.

"You guys are so mediocre compared to us. Fucking yuppies! Now give me my money!"

"It's not your money. I'm taking what you owe us out of the deposit."

Vicki walked over to the phone and called the cops.

"Hello, yes, I live at the corner of Haight and Ashbury," she said, "and my roommates refuse to pay me my damage deposit. We're just two girls, and this guy has been really violent to us. He's been throwing chairs around and breaking our stuff. He's threatened to hurt us on a number of occasions. I think he's kind of unstable."

She hung up the phone and turned around with an evil smile on her face.

"They said they'd send a man right over."

The cop was a bumpkin version of Gomer Pyle. An idiot with a badge who thought the gun gave him the same intellectual merit as a college diploma. When we let him in we were both calm. He asked what was going on. Vicki lapsed into her 'woe is me I'm just a poor little girl and these evil guys are beating up on me' act. The cop lapped it up to the full extent of his canine gullibility. When I explained that she had caused a lot of damage to the apartment that we wanted to receive compensation for, it was obvious that he wasn't listening. After we had both said our spiels the cop said, "Well, I think you should pay her the money."

"Do you know anything about San Francisco rental law?" I asked.

"No," the officer said, "but I believe her, and I'm going to make sure you pay her by midnight."

"But according to the law, we have two weeks before we have to refund her damage deposit."

"That might be what the law says," the officer said, "but I think it sounds fair if you pay her by midnight. And I'm going to try to see that it happens."

As he left, Vicki was all smiles as she took down the number he could be reached at later that night. Nothing like having your legal rights stomped all over by a chauvinist pig.

This incident gave Vicki an open chance to scream at us as much as she wanted in the belief that the Law was behind her. For nearly an hour she degraded me nonstop, going into explicit detail about my sexual habits and a long list of hallucinatory deviations I could never even have imagined. She was trying to push me to the point where I would hit her, but I wasn't about to sink to that level. One little love tap and she'd be on the phone to Joe Macho Cop and there I'd be in a holding tank while she moved out with all my stuff as well as her own. No way I was gonna let that happen. But as she screamed on nonstop in that voice like breaking glass and fingers scratching down a blackboard, I felt myself being pushed to a point where violence would be an option too pleasurable to avoid.

Thank God, Chaos was there. Whenever our arguments reached a screaming pitch, he would walk out of my room and stand between us so it wouldn't come to blows. He remained calm as he explained to Vicki that she was nothing but a piece of white trash, and that if she wanted her money by midnight she also had to be completely moved out by that time.

"Anything that remains in the house after midnight becomes our property," Chaos concluded.

"Who the fuck are you?" Vicki screamed at him. "You show up out of nowhere and think you can tell me what to do, where do you get off at?"

"I'm a friend of John's, and I'm looking out for him," Chaos said. "I'm a buffer zone between you two. It doesn't really matter who I am, but what I do. My name's Chaos, and I'm even more chaos than you can create."

"This fuckin' mystery man shows up outta nowhere, thinks he can tell me what to do," she rambled. "Well, no one tells me what to do. He's probably a fucking yuppie too. They're all a bunch of fucking yuppies. Fucking yuppies just don't understand artists like me."

"Vicki," I said, "you don't paint or draw or make sculpture; you don't write. You tried to play music but you were so bad you got kicked out of a noise band. You're not an artist because you don't create anything."

"You wouldn't understand my art," she hissed.

"It's very easy to understand nothing," I said. "All you do is talk a lot. You dress funny but you have no creativity.

122

You don't actually do anything. You're a hanger on, a scenester, someone who clings to the fringes but contributes nothing."

"You bastard! I've been all over the world, I've eaten dinner with kings and sheiks..."

"And now you're almost homeless, you've been fired from your job, and have to steal food stamps from your best friend just to stay alive."

"I had more experiences by the time I was twenty than you'll ever have in your whole life. I fucked great artists, lived in expensive hotels, was driven around in private limousines."

"Where are the limousines now?" I said with a smile. "Why isn't one helping you move out into an expensive hotel? Huh? You're getting kind of quiet there, Vicki. Where are your rich friends and all the artists who want to fuck you? I don't think you've gotten any for at least three months. Huh, Vicki? Where are the private limousines now?"

Vicki put her head down and began sobbing, and even though it was completely evil, I felt good.

As the night progressed Vicki got more vicious, spitting blood and putrid carrot juice as she groaned and stumbled among the tattered remnants of her possessions. Her bright red gums had almost rotted through and each spit was dark brown. With breath so foul not even a fly would have kissed her, her mouth fumed like a fetid cauldron of week old garlic and spoiled fish. The knee she had smashed at the Pus Cocktail show was getting worse and worse. Now the wound had swelled up puffy and black as a toadstool, and without health insurance benefits, she was forced to hobble about on a gnarled cane as the limb grew steadily more useless. She spit on the walls constantly, and only relieved herself in the guest room corner, creating an excremental pile that had to be shoveled up, and still left a stain and smell for weeks afterwards.

Sometimes she would cut her arms with a razor blade, shaping the abrasions into occult symbols. Before they scabbed over, Kidney would daub them up with parchment, creating blood transfers that she would cross reference with the movements of the stars and satanic charts, creating, no doubt, a conjuring network for my doom. But spirits be damned, they were physically leaving my house.

It was a true a territorial struggle, animal versus animal over the same burrow space, a matter of pure evolution, three humans acting out a savage satire of Darwin's Theory. I helped them pack, roughly stuffing broken pieces of occult bric-a-brac into plastic garbage bags. I made no attempt to separate their stuff from the trash already on the floor, it was all the same to me, and even if I had tried I couldn't have told the two apart. A few bags were packed with a dust pan. As I packed I noticed how much of the stuff couldn't have been theirs. Thousands of dollars worth of clothing in sizes not even remote to the girls' measurements. Hundreds of trinkets such as gild framed photos of people they could not have known, kewpie dolls, stuffed animals, mood rings, and plastic models, a flood of personal items delineating a range of character greater than both of them could encompass. Billy Zygote had told me that witches often steal items of sentimental value to their victims in order to employ them as lenses for focusing malevolent spells. It was with an admixture of horror and relief that I noticed that none of the tiny baubles belonged to me. Or maybe they had been sure to move my trinkets out first, before I could stumble across them in the hecticness of the move.

God, there I was, Mister Secular Humanist, beginning to worry about magic. These women were driving me crazy. Since their arrival my stress level had gone through the roof, my work performance was dropping steadily, every time I left the house I became obsessed with what would have gone wrong in my absence. I wanted nothing more than to just leave the place, and yet my worry and paranoia made me a constant prisoner of it. Since I couldn't escape it even in my mind, I would stay and fight till it was cleaned up and mine.

The stress level had even gotten to Chaos. He paced around constantly, unable to read or concentrate on anything for more than a few seconds. Even watching TV was difficult. When the phone rang he would jump clear out of his chair. Every few minutes he would have to keep me and Vicki from clawing at each other's throats. As the night went on, his face was drenched in sweat and his eyes had a distracted look, as if he were trying to cover the fact that beneath that calm expression he was violently clenching his teeth. Kidney ran up the hallway with a pluming incense censer and threw a handful of dead lizards at my feet just as I had convinced Vicki to pay at least the electric bill. She immediately tore up her check, claiming the dead reptiles as a justifying omen. I raised my fist to hit her. Chaos ran down the hall and grabbed my wrist. I tried to struggle free, my hands reaching in strangling gestures, it had gone that far. "Please," I begged Chaos, "let me go, a hundred years in jail is worth just one bloody nose."

"No," he said firmly. "If you stoop to violence their spells will begin to work."

But I didn't care anymore. My mind was a red smear, a snarling of animal teeth. Vicki began to work on Chaos.

"Look at Mr. Little Dick," she hissed. "Probably hasn't gotten a piece in two years."

I cringed. It had been about a year since he'd been laid.

"Every time he pulls his pants down the little girls laugh," she continued.

"You'd give me a blow job but all your teeth would fall out," he said with light humor.

"Well, I bet you loved a girl once," she said. "Loved her long and lived with her for two years. It was a good thing, you all fucked every morning before you even got out of bed. Yeah, it was real good. But then she left you. Just up and left. Poof. Cause one morning you woke up and your little thing had shriveled up and blown away," she laughed like a jackal.

Chaos stood there smiling, completely unaffected. He'd never lived with anyone.

"And after that," she continued, "you let old fags fuck you up the butt. They burned up that ass till it looked like an old used pussy. And then dogs walking down the street would smell your stinky old hole and come running, and you'd get down on all fours and let them fuck you like a stray bitch. Even giant roaches and slugs would crawl up out of the New York sewers and you'd bend over for them too."

She was completely crazy. Totally ludicrous. Chaos stood there smiling, his eyes full of sympathy for this lost soul. Poor girl, he seemed to be thinking, she can't help it.

And then he hit her as hard as he could. So hard she flew back against the wall, shattering plaster. He had her down on the floor, his hands in a death grip around her neck, the throat skin rippling between his fingers, turning red as her gums.

I should have jumped in and stopped them, but something held me back. Something primal and pure was going on between them.

In a voice of steel ice Chaos said, "You don't know who I am. I could kill you right now. No one would ever know my name, or where I went, or what exactly happened. I'd just disappear. I'm all over this city, like a shadow, the fog, or a rumor. Wherever you go in this town from now on, I want you to know that I'll be right behind you. You might not see me, but I'll be there. And I could get you at any time. You see, I really am Chaos. And I love you."

He kissed her very gently on the lips. Then his hands sprang away from her neck as if they had never been there. Vicki was too dazed to even cry. Regaining my senses, I dragged Chaos down the hallway into my room.

"You cracked," I spit out in a hoarse whisper. "After all your talk of inner strength and control, you cracked. You let her get through to you."

"As soon as I hit her I got an erection," he said.

"You're sick."

"I couldn't help it."

"These women make everyone around them sick."

"In a horrible way it was one of the most profound sexual moments of my life," he said sheepishly. "I'll probably jerk off thinking about it."

"Don't ever tell anyone this, Chaos, but I'm glad you did it. I couldn't do it. But somebody had to."

"I think she wanted it this way," Chaos whispered in a voice helpless and used.

"I think so too. Did you notice how calm she was after it happened? And listen... Nothing. Silence. She's stopped screaming for the first time today."

"Look buddy, you're on your own now," Chaos said. "It's time for me to fade back into the night. And you're not going to see my face around these parts for awhile. But before I go I want you to get something straight. Nothing happened. Got it? Nothing occurred here tonight."

I nodded my head. "Got it. Nothing at all. Nada. I don't even know you. Haven't even heard your name before." "You watch yourself. You got some serious shit going down with these girls. They pulled some things up outta me I didn't even know existed. I don't know if it's magic or the devil, but they brought something bad into this household. Be careful. Now I gotta go get me some serious psychotherapy. Good luck." And he slipped out the back door.

For a second I just stood there, staring into the mirror, realizing that some subtle, almost invisible change had occurred in the face that gazed back at me. A tiny nuance had been shifted and now everything was different. I had been poisoned by the whole affair. Like a slow rot that ate all the way down to the core of my being, I knew I could never look at women in the same way again. A raw side of the female psyche had been revealed to me that I could never have imagined existed. And I was terrified of it. Terrified to such a degree that I would be watchful of it till my dying day.

On that last day when they finally moved out for good, Billy Zygote showed up to help Kidney move out. I didn't care what his motives were, he was just pushing Kidney in the right direction - out my front door. As far as I was concerned, he could cut her head off once she was on the street. She had so much stuff, trunks and boxes full of belongings, carloads and carloads of tattered junk.

"You know," said Billy as we were hustling out a chest of drawers, "this is the third or fourth time I've helped Kidney move and she has more stuff every time. One time I was carrying out this trunk of hers, it was so fucking heavy, must've weighed over three hundred pounds. When I get it out on the street and open it up, it's all full of anchors. I was gonna throw them away, but Kidney was like, 'Don't you dare! I've been working years on my anchor collection.' The next time I move her, she has a trunk that's even heavier, and when I open that, it's all full of bricks. It was her brick collection."

"People who are homeless shouldn't be collecting bricks and anchors," I said.

JOIN TOGETHER

The way things join together into other things is so amazing to the strange breakdown of words, arrange these sentences as you please, please make some message through the haze of words that join together, tear apart strange, make a graze of words, eat grass of sounds, smash right daze, a glaze of haze, crazed never coming back, lost in the words that move and talk around all things on the radio, on the TV, the news is all words drifting through societies like a haze, a glaze on the harsh edges, words are how we lubricate things, the ugly things we make them sing, dress them pretty in words, keep that haze going, don't stop talking or the time, the heart, all things will stop the haze, keep the haze going, pump it full of words make them strong, make them sing, sing long till your lungs stop because words is all we are, we are ideas, phrases, groups of stories, things never said, we keep talking and only the dead are silent, but they keep talking in us and we keep talking about them and even the dead talk in words that keep moving, changing, growing into each other, words are something alive and even once all matter is gone hopefully the words will keep moving, a sound that still goes on, into some darkness, the darkness the words keep away.